Full Circle

Endwell Investigations, Volume 1

fj donohue

Published by Frank Donohue, 2023.

FULL CIRCLE

First edition. February 1, 2023.

ISBN: 979-8215179871

Written by fj donohue.

Full Circle
An Endwell Investigations Mystery
By
FJ Donohue

Chapter 1

Raymond Leonard was twenty-three years old and autistic, high functioning but not able to live on his own. However, he was able to interact with other people and maintain social relationships. He lived with his mother and father on Binghamton's west-side and worked at The Sheltered Workshop in town. His brother was a senior at Northeastern University in Boston majoring in statistics. He planned to stay in the Boston area after graduation.

It was a safe and comfortable life for Raymond. He had his family, his job and his home. His parents helped him to develop his independence. They knew that there would come a day when they would not be able to look after him. Along with his father, he managed the day-to-day household expenses. He had a number of other jobs around the house, all designed to help him understand what it took to run a house and be independent. Although he did not drive, he did most of the grocery shopping for the family. There was a Weis supermarket about five blocks from the house. He had a backpack and roller cart he used to carry the groceries. He enjoyed the structure of shopping. Make a list, go to the store, buy the groceries, take them home and then put them away. The completeness of the task was appealing to him. A defined beginning and end.

He was also a bit of an explorer. His trips were not always a straight walk to the store but a wider-ranging walk about the town. When he was little, his mom had always pointed out the trees and flowers when they went on their walks, and he still liked to look at them.

The season was well into fall. The clocks had been turned back and the days were much shorter now. There were plenty of leaves still on the trees but their earlier vibrant colors were now dull and they would soon fall. Raymond had decided to take a walk to look at the leaves on the way to the store because he'd heard his mom say they'd soon be gone.

This evening, he walked through an older part of Binghamton that had seen better days but where the trees were fully grown. The city was trying to improve the area and some of the abandoned houses had been torn down.

He was passing two empty lots, side by side. They had been there for some time and were overgrown, neighborhood junk starting to accumulate. He casually stopped and walked in a bit to look around. But the vegetation was dense and in the fading light he couldn't see much. As he was leaving the lot to continue his walk, he saw three men having a heated conversation in the back of the lot. He saw flashes and heard the sound of gunshots. Two men had been shot and he saw it happen!

Raymond was terrified. *What just happened?* he thought. Then he saw a man with a gun coming toward him. Without knowing what he was doing or where he was going, he quickly ran out of the lot, crossed the street and headed towards the downtown area. *I have to get away! This is a really bad man,* was all he could think.

But Raymond was not the only one on the street. Reilly Harrington, who was from Rochester, had arrived at the bus station earlier and was on his way to the same lot to pick up a backpack full of drugs. He had been sober for some months now and was trying to get away from the drug life. However, the lure of some quick money was hard to resist. So, he thought, one more trip as a drug mule for a dealer in the Rochester area and then close it out. Reilly made most of his trips in upstate New York, with occasional runs to New York

City. Being a drug mule supported his meager lifestyle. He knew this type of work was reckless and dangerous. Sooner or later it would come crashing down on him.

When he arrived at the lot to pick up the drugs, Raymond was already gone and all he saw was a guy running down the street with a gun. It wasn't anyone he knew. *Whoa, that's not one of the dudes I'm supposed to meet. Where are my guys?,* thought Reilly. He knew something was wrong. Really wrong! He went up to the lot and looked in but couldn't see much. He went into the lot about ten feet and then he saw the two guys he was supposed to meet, both dead. *I got to get out of here now! Somebody must have heard something. I don't want to be around when the cops come.* He quickly got out of the lot and headed downtown. He headed back to the bus station looking for the next bus to Rochester. *Someone robbed those guys and killed them. He'll shoot me, to, if he knows I was there.*

Raymond had stopped running now. He walked at a rapid pace but where to go? He came to the bus station and saw three buses loading and unloading. *I'll take one of those buses. I have to get out of here now. If the bad man finds me, he'll hurt me!*

Raymond had the grocery shopping money and some of his own. Not much, maybe sixty dollars total. Small bills and change. He went up to the ticket window and just looked at the agent. He didn't know what to say. Where should he go? He looked back at the buses at the gates and thought, *one of these I guess.*

He was looking at the Rochester bus when the ticket agent said, "What's it going to be my friend?"

"That one, Rochester," replied Raymond.

"Can't do that, it just came in from Rochester and will depart in ten minutes for Monticello and then on to the city. There is a Rochester bus coming from the city in thirty minutes." New York City was usually referred to as the city by the upstate folks.

"Want that one?"

"Okay," replied Raymond. "I'll take that bus."

"It'll go from Gate 3 over there; we'll make an announcement soon."

Raymond bought a ticket and took a seat near Gate 3 where he could see most of the doors in the terminal and waited for the bus.

Reilly Harrington came into the bus station about ten minutes after Raymond sat down. He went up to the ticket window. "When's the next bus to Rochester?"

"The driver just called in with a status. He's about fifteen minutes out. Want a ticket?"

"Yeah."

Reilly paid for the ticket, sat down to wait for the incoming bus. *What is going on? That's it, I'm finished with this life. If I'd been in that lot ten minutes earlier, I'd be toast. It's over! Maria is right, sooner or later you die in the drug business. I'm going to continue to stay sober this time and not go back. If the killer knows I was nearby, he'll find me and kill me for sure.* Maria Suarez was Reilly's on-again-off-again girlfriend. Reilly wanted a more committed relationship but she would not get too close to him given his life style. She was there for him but would not let the relationship develop. She worked as an administrator at a not-for-profit that supported halfway houses in Rochester and Monroe County. Mainly for people recently released from prison or enrolled in rehabilitation programs.

Reilly texted his dealer in Rochester. They had a codeword system to let him know he had picked up the "package" and also if he had trouble. Reilly used a burner and sent a text with the codewords for a problem. It said, "gone south 11:50" which was the code for a broken deal and the arrival time in Rochester for his bus. He took the sim card out of the burner and broke it into small pieces. He knew he'd have a reception committee waiting for him when he got to Rochester. *These guys have only one way to deal with problems—violence! They're not going to be happy campers,* he thought.

As he was sitting in the station lobby, he noticed Raymond sitting not too far away. He looked agitated and clearly in a very nervous state. He was constantly rocking forward and back which Reilly knew was a coping mechanism for extreme stress. *Well, I guess I'm not the only guy with problems. This dude is hurting,* he thought. Reilly kept looking at Raymond. It was odd; he was not dressed as a typical guy would be at his age. The clothes were clean and not worn but there was a style and color disconnect. Sort of like his mother was still buying his clothes. The colors and styles were a bit dated. If he was aware of it, it didn't seem to bother him. At that point, they made eye contact. Reilly felt sorry for the guy. He smiled and made a small hand wave gesture. Raymond didn't respond but kept looking in his direction. *Strange dude,* thought Reilly, *wonder what his problem is?* He guessed he was five to ten years older than Raymond. Neither one knew that the other had been way too close to the murders.

When they started to board the Rochester bus, Reilly was one of first to board. He took a seat by a window. The bus was about half full. He saw Raymond still outside. He was letting the other passengers board ahead of him. *Is this guy going to get on the bus? He really seems confused,* he thought.

About that time the bus driver was coming out of the terminal with the passenger manifest and spoke to Raymond. Reilly couldn't hear what was said but imagined he was telling him to board the bus if he wanted to go to Rochester. Raymond got on the bus; spotted Reilly and sat down next to him. *What the hell, plenty of empty seats, why sit next to me? What's your game?* They settled in to their seats and were off to Rochester. Reilly could sense Raymond constantly looking at him as he kept rocking back and forth.

Finally Raymond said, "I'm Raymond. I'm going to Rochester."

"Well, you're on the right bus. Is someone going to meet you?"

"I don't have anybody."

"Where are you going to stay?"

"I don't have anybody."

"You already said that. You can't just get on a bus and get someplace at midnight without a place to stay and a plan."

What am I going to do about this guy? thought Reilly, *I just can't cut him loose at the bus station at midnight. Nothing good will come from that. Maybe I should keep him for the night and then get social services involved tomorrow. I'll call Maria and see what she thinks. Something's not right with this guy and I don't understand it. He's not a threat but he acts sort of strange. Christ, when is all this shit going to end? The Rochester dealers are going to be really pissed off at losing their dope and will try to blame me for it. I can see that coming. Now I got this weird dude who doesn't have a clue about what he's doing.*

Chapter 2

How long has it been? he thought. Today was a special day. It was the anniversary of Emi's and the baby's murder all those years ago. Anniversary? Isn't that for a celebration? Should be a happy time; but for Alastair, it was a day of remembrance. He always made sure the day was spent quietly away from his busy private investigation agency. He sat quietly in his house in Endwell, New York thinking back to those days as he always did every year on this day.

The events were still with him. Not so much the trauma now but certainly the memory. Over the years, he would hear a laugh, voice intonation, see a color and it would trigger memories. Although Alastair, known to his friends as Al, had never been in combat, he knew that this is what PTSD must be like. Most of the memories now were from the good times they had together. The memories of the trauma were still there but he had learned to manage them and live with them.

What happened back then?

Alastair had majored in Finance and Economics in college. He joined the Air Force and was an Electronics Officer in the Air Force. Go figure that. The needs of the Air Force trumped any career path you had in mind! However, it was a good maturing process for him. Command of a large team at various detachments around the world and a department head when back at the home base.

He got out of the Air Force after four years and joined the FBI. They liked his college major and Air Force background. It was a good fit for them and for Alastair. After training at Quantico, VA, he was assigned to the field office in Houston as part of a team chasing an entrenched money laundering operation. It took three years to assemble the case, but when they finished, it was bullet-proof. All the bad boys went down!

Alastair was a very good investigator and analyst. He had established himself with the bureau. After his success in Houston, he was promoted and posted to the field office in Miami. A bigger operation and more action. He headed a team of four agents investigating a drug and money laundering operation with hooks into other east coast states. This was a lot more complicated and like the Houston operation, would not be solved overnight.

His new boss, Chris Collins, summarized the job best. "Al, Miami is just like Houston, no home runs here either. Singles and doubles are good. Hell, I'll even take a base on balls!"

"I understand Chris, dig, dig, dig."

"You got that right! But before you start on the case, take a few days and find yourself a nice place to live. Miami has all kinds of residential pockets, so to say. Smaller neighborhoods where folks sort of know each other. Let me ask my wife to show you around, it'll take some of the mystery out of it."

He found a nice condominium about twenty minutes from the office. It was at the bottom of a cul-de-sac. Six buildings with four apartments in each building. Plenty of trees and green space. Good shopping nearby. *This is really nice*, he thought. *Am I with the FBI for the long haul? Maybe.*

Three years later, it all came crashing down!

Chapter 3

Not long after he arrived in town, Alastair met Emily McDougal at the University of Miami. He was at the university library looking for language training material and online courses. Before coming to Miami, the bureau had sent him to Quantico to learn Italian. A lot of the bad boys he was interested in spoke Italian and the bureau wanted him to get closer to their language and culture. He found he had a good aptitude for languages and wanted to maintain his proficiency. *I want to improve my Italian and also look into Spanish,* he thought. *Speaking Spanish will make living here a lot more comfortable. They're both romance languages so they share common roots. Should be an easier challenge.*

Emily was an independent editor and researcher who owned her own business. Her assignments were varied. Editing and fact checking nonfiction books and novels were the bulk of her business. She also supported the faculty at the university in their research work as well as cleaning up clumsy sentences and better organizing their reports. This part of the business was expanding rapidly. She worked out of her house about fifteen minutes from the university. She had done well with the business and was planning to take on an assistant. She was twenty-seven, closer to twenty-eight and Alastair was thirty-one, taking a hard look at thirty-two. Probably not love at first sight for either of them, but they knew this relationship was special and would grow. Both of them were long past the boy-girl dating scene. They were married about a year later.

They rented out his condo and he moved into Emily's comfortable bungalow. Like his condo, it was in a quiet area with lots of green space and trees.

One afternoon, Alastair came home early from the office. Emily had just finished editing a faculty research report on statistical theory that was poorly organized and loaded with errors in grammar. She was happy to have that behind her. She found Alastair with his head in the refrigerator looking for something to tide him over until dinner.

"Don't get your head stuck in the fridge, crime fighter! Dinner will be early tonight; I have a meeting on campus with the author of this research report I just finished. The guy may be smart but he sure can't write. Must have slept through all his English classes. Let's go out for dinner tomorrow night. I have a surprise for you and want to have a nice evening to tell you."

"Great, can you give me a hint?"

"Certainly not. You're going to have to pay to find out!"

"Will it make me happy?"

"Well, it won't make you sad, silly."

Alastair made a reservation at their favorite Italian restaurant. He had gotten to know the staff and it was always an opportunity to use his Italian. Mistakes and all! They loved him for trying and one of the waiters usually imitated his accent with much laughter. Always fun to be around friends.

They never made it to the restaurant!

He saw the big SUV in the rear mirror as it started to pass them while they drove on a causeway with water on both sides. He didn't see the rear side window come down and never saw the Uzi. They were both struck multiple times and were forced off the road, rolling over and crashing into the water.

Alastair was in a coma for more than two months. When he came around, he didn't know where he was and was in a panic to see his wife. He was in a well-lit hospital room with a wall of monitors constantly blinking and chirping. He tried to get up and one or more of the devices attached to him fell off. A nurse quickly came in to make sure he was okay. When she saw he was awake, she immediately called the attending doctor.

"Where's my wife? Where am I? What day is it?"

"The doctor will be here in a minute, Mr. Stewart."

Doctor Gilmore arrived a few minutes later. He was surprised to see Alastair conscious. Usually, a patient will exhibit some mild activity before coming out of a coma. Maybe some body movement, eye flutter or even vocal sounds. His brain activity had been active so they anticipated he would regain consciousness but this was a surprise.

Alastair asked the doctor the same questions. "Where's my wife? Where am I? What day is it?"

"I'm sorry, Mr. Stewart, your wife did not survive the attack. She died at the scene. We couldn't save the baby either. It was too early in the pregnancy."

Alastair was numb. He couldn't process the information. He just lay there trying to understand what was just said. *I can't even cry*, he thought, *what's wrong with me? What's going on? Did he say baby? That must have been the surprise she had for me. What am I going to do? I've got to get out of here and find the killer!*

"Mr. Stewart, I know you have a million questions, but for now I want you to try to put them aside and rest. I promise I'll be back and we can go into all the detail you feel you can handle. Also, Special Agent Collins will be coming by, we called him to let him know you had regained consciousness. But, for now, rest. You have a long road ahead. I don't want any other visitors for at least five days. After that we'll see what makes sense. You're safe here and we'll take good care of you."

About two days later Alastair woke up in the middle of the night. He was crying uncontrollably. The ICU nurse came in and sat next to him, just holding his hand. There were no medicines to make this better.

The next day Dr. Gilmore came to Alastair's room. "Let's talk about your injuries and the way forward."

"I don't give a shit about any of that. What happened to my wife? Where is she? She was pregnant? Where's the baby? I need to know about all of this now!"

"You're right, Mr. Stewart. I'm sorry. I wasn't thinking of your concerns. Agent Collins will fill you in on the crime issues, but let me tell you that you and your wife were ambushed on a causeway. The attacker had an automatic pistol. An Uzi, I think. He sprayed the car with bullets. One of them hit your wife in the head and killed her instantly. When she died, the baby was lost also. She was about six weeks pregnant. Your car rolled over on its side in the water and partially sank."

"A little baby, you say. Could you tell the sex?"

"I'm sorry, it was too early in the pregnancy."

"Where are my wife and baby buried?"

"Her parents buried them in their home town, Fort Walton Beach. They would like to see you when you're able. Can we talk about your condition?"

"I guess."

"You were shot multiple times. Seven in all. Your left knee was hit and severely damaged when your car went into the water. We had to put an artificial joint in your knee. Another shot hit your elbow. You had some broken ribs and a lot of infection. We have that all under control now. You're going to be with us for some time I'm afraid. We can fix all of this but you also need to work with a therapist to address the psychological side. Please consider doing this, Mr. Stewart."

"Why? There's nothing left."

"There is, Mr. Stewart, but you'll have to find it. It won't be easy."

Early the next week, Special Agent Chris Collins came to visit. Alastair was making progress. His speech and coordination were much better. However, his memory of the events was limited. He had no memory of anything after the killer started firing his gun. It was all blank. He remembered looking at the big SUV as it came up aside of him but did not remember any faces. It all exploded in a hail of bullets and shattered glass. He thought he might have some dim memories of being hit but then everything went blank.

"The doc told me Emi and I were ambushed. I don't know anything else. What happened, Chris?"

"As the Doc told you earlier, you were ambushed. We haven't caught the shooter yet. We're pretty sure it was a contract hit crew from New York City. Your investigation was starting to get very close to these guys and they wanted to put a stop to it. We got the information on the crew from an informant we know to be reliable. He didn't have any names. We don't have any video of the shooting and nothing was recovered. All the shell casings fell into their SUV. We've not been able to match any of the recovered bullets in our database. It was a clean gun."

"What's next?"

"Maybe when we shut them down, they may try to trade off the contract crew for a break in their sentences. We'll keep looking but you know how these things go. So far there isn't any talk on the streets. We need a break."

"I understand."

"Can I be candid, Al?"

"Sure, go ahead."

"You need to consider the next steps. The thinking at the office is for you to take a disability retirement. There is no way the bureau will put you in harm's way again. They just won't do it. Not after everything that happened, losing your wife and baby. You could find an analyst job in Washington or Quantico if that's what you want. Or go off in a new direction."

"I can't think about any of that now. I hurt all over and need to focus. I don't even know where to start. I just want to go to sleep and wake up to find out this was just a bad dream and never happened."

Chapter 4

When the bus arrived in Rochester, it was clear that Raymond had attached himself to Reilly. He had bonded with Reilly although he may not have understood it at the time. They were among the last passengers to get off the bus. Raymond stayed close by his side.

"Hang on a minute, I need to make a phone call," said Reilly.

Although it was close to midnight, Maria Marchetti was still up sorting out a proposal for a funding grant submittal due the next day. In her line of work, raising money was a way of life. Keep the money flow coming in and try to find new sources. Her nonprofit was successful and recognized as a valued member of the support community; so, raising money was difficult but not impossible.

"If you're in jail, Reilly, this call is finished. I can't imagine any other reason for you calling at this time of night."

"No, no, nothing like that. I just got back to Rochester from Binghamton. This guy has attached himself to me and I don't know what to do with him. He's not a druggy or anything like that but he's terrified of something."

"Is he a kid running away?"

"Well, he is trying to get away from something but he's no kid. Under twenty-five, I guess. He seems like a gentle guy but really scared. I don't know what happened to him. I also have a problem, Maria. I was in Binghamton picking up a package."

"Stop that package crap, Reilly! You were being a mule again, weren't you? I won't help you with any of that stuff. You're flying solo."

"I've been sober for six months; you know that."

"So what! Big deal! You're still working for them as their mule. Just because you're not using, you think it's okay to be their delivery boy bringing drugs and misery into Rochester. You're a dumb-ass fool!"

"Please, just meet with me and Raymond, I'm scared. I don't know what to do. I can't just leave him at the bus station."

Maria thought about it for a few minutes before answering. As always with Reilly, it was never simple. Her first thought was to cut Reilly loose and let him sort it out. But she was concerned about the person with him. He could be disabled.

"Alright, I'll meet with you and this Raymond guy but that's all. Your other life is off-limits. I don't want to know about it. Don't bring it up. If you do, I'll walk. You know that all night diner about four blocks away, Freddy's?"

"Yeah."

"I'm guessing neither of you has eaten recently. I'll meet you there and we can talk about Mr. Raymond, and you can get something to eat."

Reilly ended the call and said, "Let's go, Raymond, I've a friend who can help you. We're going to meet her at a diner nearby."

"Good, I'm hungry."

As they left the bus terminal, LaMont and his enforcer were waiting for them on the street. "Okay, asshole, we're going for a walk. I want my drugs."

The men got a firm grip on Reilly and Raymond and went down the street and then turned into a narrow alley between two buildings. "Get back there away from the street," said the enforcer.

Raymond was terrified and had started to sob. He kept moving around Reilly, not able to stay still.

"Tell that dude to be still and shut up or I'll make sure he's quiet. Who is he? You were supposed to be alone. Is this your partner in the drug heist?"

"LaMont, he has nothing to do with any of this. He attached himself to me at the Binghamton bus terminal. I'm trying to get him sorted out for the night and then turn him in to social services in the morning. I think he's retarded or something."

"I don't believe any of this shit. You go to Binghamton alone, screw up my drug deal and now show up in Rochester with this guy. I want my drugs, Reilly, or I'll take you and this guy with you apart."

"I don't have them. Someone robbed the guys in Binghamton and killed them."

"Bullshit. You were late for the meet. Get there on time and none of this would have happened. You screwed this up big time."

At that point, Lamont's enforcer hit Reilly in the face with a short, hard punch. It caught him flush on the nose and broke it. Blood splattered all over the wall. Then he hit him in the stomach and Reilly went down gasping for air. Raymond started crying loudly and was trying to get away. LaMont grabbed him and slammed him into a brick wall. He struck the wall with his head and was knocked unconscious.

LaMont said to his enforcer, "Okay, let's get out of here. Someone walking by may have heard us."

Looking down at Reilly, he said, "If I find out you were involved in the heist in Binghamton, you're dead meat. I'll find you and kill you along with that retard with you."

Reilly didn't try to answer. What could he say? He just lay there hoping for them to leave. Raymond was starting to come around and was crying softly. He was not bleeding heavily but was clearly disoriented. They sat there for a bit while Reilly tried to clean himself up. The bleeding had stopped but he had a fair amount of blood on his shirt. He had a light windbreaker with him and zipped it up to hide most of the blood.

"Come on, Raymond, we need to meet up with Maria. Let's hope she's still there."

When they got to Freddy's Diner, Maria was seated in a corner booth on the far end of the diner. The diner was a throwback to earlier days in terms of design and furnishings. Formica counter tops and vinyl covered seats in the booths. Most of the cooking was done on grills along the wall behind the counter. Freddy's had a good reputation for coffee, sausages, and home fries which were made on the premises. There were a few customers seated on counter stools. When she saw the two men, she was shocked.

"What happened? Who did this? We need to call the police."

"No, no! No cops! They'll kill us!"

"Tell me what happened and don't sugarcoat it. Damn, I said we would not talk about your drug life and here we go. If you don't get out of the life, I'm gone. No more warnings."

Reilly responded, "I was in Binghamton picking up drugs for my man here. When I got to the pickup spot, the guys I was supposed to meet were dead. Someone shot them and stole the drugs. I went right back to the bus terminal and got the next bus here. When we got back here, the dealer and his enforcer forced us into an alley and beat us up. He was really mad about the robbery in Binghamton and tried to blame it on me. Raymond was with me and they beat him up, too."

"How does Raymond figure into this?"

"He was at the Binghamton bus terminal. He was very nervous and disturbed about something. He sort of attached himself to me when we got on the bus. He's a gentle guy, not violent. Something's not right about him though. He talks okay but sometimes he's a bit odd. I don't know what's going on with him. He doesn't have much money and no idea where to go. I was thinking you could help me deal with him."

"We should call the cops," said Maria.

"Are you kidding me! We would be dead before the end of the day. These guys don't leave a trail. What am I supposed to tell the cops?

I was part of a drug deal gone bad in Binghamton and the Rochester dealer worked me over? They'll know if we go to the cops and will kill us."

Maria shifted gears and asked Raymond, "How are you feeling, Mr. Raymond? Are you hurt? Do you want to go to the hospital?"

"He didn't respond just kept looking at Reilly. Finally, he said, "My head hurts but I feel a bit better. Reilly can help me."

Maria looked back to Raymond. "Can you tell me your name?"

"I'm Raymond."

"Do you have a last name?" No response

"Where do you live?" No response

"Why are you afraid?" No response.

"Reilly, he could have a severe concussion. He should be seen by a doctor."

"Honest, Maria, I asked him the same questions in Binghamton. Same thing, no answers. Something happened to him there and he's blocked it out of his mind along with everything else. He saw something that really scared him. I want to take him to my place. We need to hide out until this blows over. If LaMont and his guys find the robber in Binghamton, I can see him trying to cut a deal and saying anything to protect his ass, including claiming we were part of the robbery. I can't take any chances now. I promise you, I'm out of this life for sure."

"I don't like this at all, Reilly. You're at risk and so is Raymond. You don't have a game plan moving forward. Okay, take him home for now and let's look at this again in the morning. This isn't going to just go away. Hiding out doesn't fix the problem. You have to get out of the drug life and maybe even leave the area. I mean what I said about this being the last time I'm getting involved."

Reilly had recently moved from Rochester to Victor, a small town just outside the city. It was a nicer place and the rents were cheaper.

"Does anyone know you just moved?"

"Not really."

"Did you leave a forwarding address?"

"I was going to stop by the old place and give one to the landlord but haven't done it yet."

"Don't. What about your mail?"

"Yeah, did it last week. Shit."

"Maybe not a problem," said Maria, "they usually don't give out your new address. They will take the mail and forward it, but the address should remain private. You should be okay. Remember, you can't go back to your old place ever. I'll give you a ride home now."

"No, we'll take a taxi. I don't know who could be watching us now. Stay here until after we leave and then go home. I'll call in a few days."

"Where's your car?"

"At the new place, I wasn't sure how long I'd be in Binghamton. Sometimes its multiple stops for the drug pickups, so I went to the bus terminal by cab."

Reilly and Raymond stayed at his new apartment for the next six weeks, only going out for groceries. Maria kept in touch with them during this time. Raymond was not seriously hurt, and his recovery was complete. Reilly spent most of the time trying to sort out the next phase of his life. So many questions to be answered he thought. *Should I stay in the area? What am I going to do? What should I do with Raymond? Too many questions and not enough answers yet. I never planned for any of this. Why is this happening to me? Is it some kind of payback for my crappy lifestyle?*

And so began the long-term relationship between the two men. Reilly, ever protective of Raymond who was happy to be with a good person who looked after him. His memory of Binghamton and the old life gone from his consciousness and over time not an ongoing source of anxiety. He seemed to only live in the present. No clear memory of the past and no plans for the future. Reilly had thought about just dropping him at the police station and let them take it from there.

But he knew that Raymond would not be able to tell them anything about his past and would end up lost in social services. He was too old for foster care. Most likely he would end up in a hospital and then be discharged with no way forward. Maybe his parents might be able to find him if he were released, but that would put Raymond right back in Binghamton in the middle of his trauma. Nothing good would come of that. Also, he worried about the killer finding Raymond's parents. They wouldn't last long if he found them. Reilly knew he couldn't cut him loose. He had to protect and take care of him. Maybe over time, things would be resolved. But for now, he was his mentor and caregiver. He was his family.

Reilly had completed two years at the University of Rochester before he fell into the dark pit of drugs. He was a good student, popular with his classmates. But drugs took him to another world, one with no easy way out. He dropped out of the University and started being a mule for the local dealers to support his habit. Maria told him he was in "Never-Never Land" and she wanted no part of it. Although they kept in touch, Maria wouldn't have anything to do with the drug side of Reilly's life or with his associates. Reilly knew that you didn't get away from drugs without paying the price. Broken relationships with friends and family, health issues and worst of all, a monkey you carried on your back for the rest of your life. A constant gnawing for the drug high and easy money.

Now he knew he had to reinvent himself and start again. Caring for Raymond opened up a side of him that he did not know existed. Helping people. It gave him a sense of peace and maybe some payback for all the grief he caused bringing drugs into Rochester.

He enrolled at Monroe Community College and got certified as a Licensed Practical Nurse or LPN as they are known. He worked as a caregiver at a local agency for a year. After that he went back to the University of Rochester and got certified as a Registered Nurse or RN. He opened up his own home care agency. Providing care filled a need and it was important to him. He worked independently providing care and over time the business prospered. He bought a small comfortable house in Victor. His agency now had twelve people on staff. He always made sure he was part of the care giving teams, not just the boss in the office. The real surprise was Raymond. He loved math and spreadsheets. The complexity of them and their ability to handle a vast amount of data was a joy to him. In the end, Raymond was the de-facto office manager. He managed the customer accounts and scheduling. The office was all digital and he loved it. The two men operated out of an office in a small strip mall in Victor. They didn't want to be trapped in their house as Reilly would say. Their small office gave them a place to go to every day and also helped Raymond develop his social skills. He thrived in this environment.

Their business was well established now. Twelve years and counting. From a humble beginning working out of his house as an independent care provider to the owner of a well-established agency with a growing client base.

The two men were a bit like chalk and cheese. So different, yet as a team, so effective. Reilly never married although he and Maria were still together and as close as Maria would allow. Both were long past the idea of marriage and a family. In many respects, Raymond was the son in their relationship. They shared the responsibility for Raymond between them. *I'm in a good place,* thought Reilly, *the business is solid, Raymond is safe, and Maria is still part of my life. Sure is a long way from the drug days. If I had stayed in that life, I'd be long dead by now.*

Reilly always wondered what happened to Raymond in those early days back in Binghamton. He tried on a number of occasions to talk about it with Raymond, but he wouldn't go there. Raymond always seemed to be in the present. No thoughts about the future and clearly no ability to address the past. *Was it a family issue? Criminal past? Always a mystery. What happened to you, Raymond?*

Chapter 5

After three major operations and months of aggressive rehabilitation Alastair was released. He had been under hospital care for six months, spending the last three months in their rehab unit next to the hospital.

Emily's parents came down from Fort Walton Beach to visit him a number of times. His sister who lived in Endwell, New York also visited. She was with him in Miami to help him settle back into his house when he was released from the hospital.

He was not even close to a decision about the next steps in his life. "Al, why don't you come back to New York and live near us," suggested his sister, "you've moved around all your life between the Air Force and FBI. You're all the family I have, and my boys would love to have you in their lives now. I can't see you staying in Miami, it'll be too painful."

"I've thought about it, Jane, but what can I do? My active investigation role with the bureau is over and I don't want to be an analyst in an office somewhere in the FBI system. I want to continue to be an investigator but after getting shot up so badly, I don't think I can hook up with any law enforcement organizations. In their eyes, I'm disabled. It's a struggle to see the next steps. What can I do? Maybe a security guard at the local mall or for a rock band!"

"Well, I know you're feeling better when you can joke about it all. But look, Al, if a career with law enforcement is not in the cards, why don't you start your own detective agency?"

"You serious?"

"Absolutely. I've even looked into it a bit. The law firms in town don't have full time investigators. Maybe up in Syracuse but not in Binghamton. They use outside resources, so I'm told. Also, insurance companies are always looking for people to validate questionable claims. Adjusters can assess the costs, but they need someone to investigate fraud. You'll probably have to do your share of documenting infidelities between couples when you start out, but you can grow the business and move away from those kinds of cases. There are two shops in town that do private work and from what I'm told, they're old school. Retired cops chasing cheating husbands and wives. Not a lot of depth there at all."

"How did you find out all of this?"

"Simple, I spoke to Brad Petronella. Remember him? He's a part time investigator for the Broome County DA and does mediations at the Resolution Center in town. He knows all about these things."

"I remember him. He was seriously wounded some years back when he was a detective with the Binghamton police. You sent me the newspaper stories."

"Sure was. He rescued his wounded partner who was being held hostage. He was shot up pretty badly. Like you, it ended his career. He still lives down the street from me."

"Hmm, let me think about it."

"Forget thinking about it, do something about it! Brad reinvented himself after he was shot up. Sound familiar? You can do that, too."

"How come you're so bossy?" laughed Alastair.

"Because, I'm your big sister and so much smarter than you!"

"What can I say? I yield to your wisdom and guidance!"

"Al, I know this is a huge gear change for you and I don't mean to make light of it. Give it some serious thought. Personally, I'd love to have my brother near me again. Your nephews Bobby and Brian talk about you all the time. Give Brad a call, he knows the lay of the land. See what he thinks."

"I'll call him. First, I need to go up to Fort Walton Beach and see Emi's parents and visit Emi's grave."

Alastair flew up to Fort Walton Beach. A short one hour and thirty-minute flight from Miami. Much better than a nine hour plus drive. He was in no shape yet for such a long drive so the flight was the logical choice. Emi's parents, Nigel and Marie met him at the airport.

"Do you want to go straight to the cemetery, Al, or have some lunch first?"

"Let's go to the cemetery first; we can talk along the way and back at the house."

"You look pretty good these days," said Nigel, "It's been three weeks since we last saw you. I can see a good change. You've come a long way, my boy."

"I guess I have, and I'm happy with the progress. I never thought I would come around. But the next steps are not clear at all. My sister wants me to go back to New York and set up my own private investigation agency. I sort of like the idea of owning my own shop. Emi ran a successful business and I learned a lot from her. I think it's the way forward but I feel I need to stay close to Emi. Am I running away?"

Marie responded, "Al, your life is in front of you, not behind you. You have to move forward and live this new life. Emily would not have wanted it any other way. You can always come back and visit, and we hope you do."

While he was in the hospital and rehab, Emi's mother had looked after their bungalow. She had a housekeeper and lawn maintenance guy there on a regular basis and a neighbor also kept an eye on the place. Alastair had a good tenant renting his condo. Marie kept an eye on that also. That side of his life was in good shape. No house or condo worries.

Alastair laughed, "Now I know where Emi got her attention to detail. Marie, you should have been a researcher and editor, too."

"You know, I just might do that. Some of Emi's clients asked me if I knew of anyone to finish up her projects. I looked them over and decided I could handle a lot of them. Maybe I'll keep it going. I can easily work out of the house here and with Nigel retired and golfing all the time, it all seems to fit. I really like editing novels and frankly, fixing up faculty research papers is enjoyable. I took Emi's files, computer and printer back here to finish up her assignments. The business has kept on growing. Old clients and new ones now. So, who knows? You open up a private investigation agency in New York and I'll carry on Emi's business here. It'll be a good move for both of us."

Nigel laughed, "Marie and Emi are the only ones who ever made sense in this family. I'm along for the ride!"

The visit to the cemetery was on a warm sunny day with a constant breeze off the Gulf of Mexico. The weather had not turned too warm yet, a good day to be outside. It was an emotional time for the three of them. Nigel and Marie held back as Alastair went forward to Emi's grave. He stood by her grave, his mind full of thoughts and memories. This was the first time Alastair had been close to Emi since the murder. As he stood there, he could feel her presence. So close, yet so far away. Never coming back. He stood quietly thinking, *Oh, Emi, what have I done? You didn't deserve this. My life and job killed you. I should never have been part of your life. You deserved much better than me. Can you ever forgive me? Two lives lost and for what? I never understood the risks of the job. I always thought it was just me at risk. Not true. Help me, Emi, I'm not sure I can carry this load. I feel so guilty for all that has happened. I lost you and the baby; and for what? Chasing a bunch of gangsters who will lawyer up and maybe even get away with it.*

After fifteen minutes or so he turned and asked Nigel and Marie to join him. The three of them stood by the grave holding hands. Marie in the middle with the men on each side. They stood there, nobody talking, all lost in their thoughts. Alastair sobbing quietly. After some time, he asked, "Where's the baby buried?"

"With Emi," replied Marie.

"Thanks, I was having a recurring dream that the baby had been disposed of by the hospital. It was so early in the pregnancy."

Marie said, "Not to worry, the hospital staff were so thoughtful. They called me after the autopsy to ask what my wishes were and candidly, I was at a loss as to what to do. They suggested that the baby stay with Emi and they be buried together."

After an hour or so, they drove back to the house and spent the remainder of the day and evening talking about things past and future. Alastair knew it would take a long time to understand everything that happened. He was happy for the time spent with Nigel and Marie. They had all been through so much these past months. Just being together was a source of comfort for the three of them. During the visit, Nigel didn't say very much but it was clear the toll that these months had taken on him. He'd lost his little girl.

Chapter 6

Once back at the house in Miami, Alastair kept walking around the place with no clear objective in mind. The house had been well looked after and there was really nothing to do. But, he just couldn't settle. *I should be doing something,* he thought. *But what?* The house was neat and clean yet so empty and quiet. Emi always had soft background music on when she was working. He loved coming into the house to be met with a warm hello and hearing the music. Now, just dead silence. Emi and the baby were gone. This part of his life was over. Other than a couple of meetings at the FBI field office to close out his case work and review his disability retirement, it was over. *It really is time to start a new chapter, if that's what it's called. I have to see this through and not spend the rest of my life feeling sorry for myself,* he thought.

The final meeting at the field office to close out his employment was a surprise. He expected to stop by, sign off his case files and pick up the paperwork regarding his disability retirement. *Not so quick there, mister!* His boss, Chris Collins, had reserved the large briefing room. It had a capacity for sixty or so people and it was definitely full. When Alastair walked in he was greeting by a sustained round of applause and a rousing cheer led by Chris. The field office director, Larry Montana, gave Alastair a citation signed by the Director General in Washington. Lunch was catered and nobody was in a hurry to leave. There was a good selection of wine and beer; a bit of a break from the conservative

Bureau policy. *I'm going to miss this life, but it's definitely over. It's time to move on. I think I'm ready now,* thought Alastair.

Later that week, he called Brad Petronella on his mobile. He was at the Resolution Center in Binghamton finishing up paperwork from a recent mediation.

"Brad, this is Al Stewart, remember me?"

"Sure, your sister told me you might call. I'm so sorry for your loss. You've been through some hard times, my friend. It's never easy."

"I seem to be coping a lot better now. Thanks for the kind thoughts. Do you have some time to talk about my next steps? I know Jane spoke to you about me opening up a shop in Binghamton."

"Actually, we've talked quite a bit about it these past three months. I like the idea."

"Do you think it will work? It seems like such a big change. Right now, I'd be more comfortable jumping off the State Street bridge downtown by the arena!"

"I think you could make a good go of it. Your background is impressive and there's a need for the service. You check all the boxes. You're going to have to spend some money upfront to set up the shop and it will be some time before you get the money back. The word has to get around and this always takes some time. I know a few folks here and can help jumpstart the business. I think you'll surprise yourself."

"I've got the resources and can spend the time and money to build this up. Money doesn't seem to be an issue at this point. We had a healthy bank account and my disability retirement is very good."

The two men spent the next forty-five minutes discussing the business model, office issues and technical support in town. Alastair knew from his FBI days that you need a good technical base to do solid research. You can't just troll around the internet hoping Google will provide the answer. He would have to subscribe to a good software research database and hire someone who understood how to use it.

They agreed to meet when he got back to Binghamton, most likely early next month, and continue the conversation.

With the good vibes from Brad, he called his sister who was back in New York. "Okay, big sister, I'm going to give setting up an agency in town a shot. Brad was very helpful. I can see a way forward."

"I'm so happy for you and my boys will be thrilled. With Ed not in my life anymore, I'm glad to have a man in their lives."

Jane had been divorced for over eight years now. She enjoyed a good relationship with her ex-husband, but Ed lived in Pittsburgh and his visits were becoming sporadic. He loved the boys but now there were other people competing for his time and attention. Like Jane, he had not remarried but with the time since their divorce, she could see the relationship between Ed and the boys changing. Less frequent calls and visits now.

"We've plenty of space here, Al, you can use the spare bedroom. The boys are still bunking together."

"You sure? It may be a couple of months, probably more. I need to find a place to live and sort out office space. On top of that, I need to find someone to run the office and manage the research on cases."

"Don't worry about it. This is a big house. You can use Ed's office in the basement to start the business. There's no panic to get an office as soon as you hit town. Use the furniture and toss out the stuff you don't need. The office is long overdue for a clean out. You'd be doing me a favor. I've done nothing with it since Ed left. The boys play games there but that's about all. It has a private entrance off the driveway so you can come and go as you want and meet with your customers. Or is it clients?"

"I like clients better. Sounds more professional. Customers sound more like retail. I should be with you at the end of the month. I'm pretty well sorted out here. I'm selling the house and keeping the condo. I'll bring the stuff I'll need on a daily basis with me in the car. You know, clothes and computer gear. I'll have a moving company bring the rest of the stuff and store it nearby."

"I'll get you a large storage unit at Laing's on North Street in Endwell. It's an established operation with good security. It's not far from my house and the boys can help you move and organize it all. You'll love your nephew Bobby, he's the detail man in the family! Where around the town are you thinking of setting up shop?"

"I don't have a clue. I need to speak with Brad about it and take some time to look around."

"Makes sense. As I said, use Ed's office until you find a good place. No rush in moving on. Put your main effort into building a client base. The office is secondary."

Alastair called Brad to let him know when he would be back in town. Along with setting up a meeting, he wanted to bounce office ideas off him. "I'm sort of up in the air about an office and location. I wonder what makes the best sense."

"Well, in my opinion, the location is not what will grow the business. Everything is fifteen minutes from everything else here. Your reputation will be the driver in establishing the business. Personally, I like Endwell. It's in the middle of the other villages and towns and easily accessible. Something with a discreet location and private access would work."

"I like Endwell, too. My sister lives there. You know, Brad, If I do end up there, I'm going to call the agency ENDWELL INVESTIGATIONS," laughed Alastair. "Nobody will know if I'm referring to the location or the results of my work."

"Endwell Investigations! I like it!" said Brad.

Alastair took his time driving back to New York. His recovery had gone well but long hours behind the wheel were not a good idea yet. He stopped near Myrtle Beach in South Carolina and spent three days at a golf resort. He played two rounds of golf and was pleasantly surprised at his level of play. *Maybe I've got some game left?* Emi's mother cautioned him to not get into a rut and to develop a social life. Find an outlet. *Golf?* It was an enjoyable couple of days for him. Comfortable room, excellent restaurants and a great golf course. He made an overnight stop around Silver Spring, Maryland and then, on up to Endwell.

He had to register with New York State as a private investigator and also get a carry permit for his pistol. Coming from the FBI, the gun approval process would be a lot easier. *I'll keep it in a small safe and go to a range occasionally just to keep some level of skill.* He never had to draw his weapon during his FBI days and didn't expect to need it as a private investigator.

He had spoken to Jane and Brad about his need for a good researcher/office manager. Both of them were on the lookout for a good candidate.

It didn't take very long. "Al, I took a training course at SUNY-Broome last month for some new software we bought for the firm. They hired a woman from the college to teach us how to use and maintain it. She's really good. Woefully unappreciated at the college. She's an adjunct," said Jane.

Alastair laughed, "You mean an academic slave laborer!"

"You got it, Mr. Investigator, you got to love the universities. Always preaching social justice and yet coveting their money. All talk, no action."

Jane worked for Baker, Bright and Colson, a medium size law firm in Binghamton. She was their office manager and software "fixer" as she like to call it. The firm was pretty much an all-digital operation. Always upgrading and adding new software. Jane was the person who evaluated it and implemented the new systems. Recently, they had purchased a new software program to allow for better tracking of recent changes in the law and case research. The standard bookcases full of law books in the firm's library were mostly for show now. The real work was done through software. A good search engine opened up a new world.

When her firm purchased the software. Jane attended a comprehensive ten-day course along with five other people from the area whose law firms had also acquired the software package. The instructor was a young woman in her early thirties. She taught computer science courses at the college every semester and was a partner in a computer repair shop in Endicott. Her role in the shop was more of an on-call advisor and technical support engineer. She didn't take any salary for her work, but got a percentage of the profits at year's end. It was a good arrangement. The two guys who ran the shop were more than happy to have access to her skills and could not afford to have her with them on a full-time basis. She worked out of her house and didn't have to spend a lot of time at the shop. If she did have to go in to work on a hardware issue, she could do it at night or on the weekend.

"She's coming to our office next week to work on some software updates, can I put you two together?" said Jane.

"Sure, I'll be in Endicott at the end of next week. Any time after that is fine with me. I can't see taking anyone on full time yet, I don't even have a client."

"Talk with her, see if anything fits. If you don't go fishing, you won't catch anything."

"You're right, let's do it."

Chapter 7

Alastair interviewed Chantal Perdue about two weeks after he arrived in Endwell. By that time his home office was set up, thanks to nephew Bobby's help and organizational skills. He had just received his Private Investigator's license so he was good to go as his nephews liked to say. Brad had done a bit of advance legwork for him. So, he opened for business with two active cases. A surveillance of a cheating husband and a questionable insurance claim. Not the top end of the investigation spectrum but a start. Brad also gave him a listing of the attorneys in the area that he obtained from the Bar Association and a list of insurance agencies and agents. Alastair was in the process of mailing out an introductory letter letting them all know he was open for business.

Chantal certainly had all the computer and research skills he needed for the agency but he didn't have the client base to pay her a salary and candidly, no case load yet to keep her busy and involved. Her response to the problem was practical and a win-win for both of them.

"Look, Mr. Stewart, I'll work for you on-call initially. Sort of like what I do for the computer shop. When you need me, give me a call and I'll work the assignments. Once the business develops, we can take the next steps."

"Good idea. By the way, please call me Al. Let me ask you a personal question. In this business there are times when it is better for a woman to do the surveillance on a case. I don't think it'll be an everyday occurrence but it will happen. Is this something you could do? I'll never put you at risk."

"Not a problem. I'm intrigued by your business and would like a role on the operational side."

"Okay, we'll need to get you a Private Investigator's license to keep it all kosher. I'll teach you the surveillance techniques and procedures. We'll work together initially, before you go solo."

And this was the start of Endwell Investigations almost ten years ago. It only took a year to get the business launched to the point where he could bring Chantal on full time and acquire an office. In the end, he bought a small building on North Street in Endwell. It was a two-story building with a barber shop and flower shop on the ground floor. Both businesses were well established having been there for a number of years. Alastair's offices were on the second floor. The parking for his agency was in the rear of the building with a private entrance. If you didn't know he was there, you'd never find him. He lived with Jane and the boys for almost two years before buying a house in Endwell near Highland Park. It was a simple raised ranch with a backyard that bordered on county land. Comfortable and quiet.

Decorating his house was a family affair. Between Jane and her boys, they had a lot of fun furnishing the house. The boys insisted that Alastair have a man-cave in the finished basement. Large screen TV and comfortable reclining chairs. A wet bar was installed along one of the walls. The boys made sure a high-speed internet connection was installed. At least as good as the one in his office so they could play their video games. One of the bedrooms was set up for the boys as they were often over to his house. If it was late, it was much easier for the boys to stay with him. Jane took care of the kitchen layout and appliances. He was more than happy to turn that chore over to someone else.

The result was a warm comfortable house. A place he liked to call home. Alastair had not remarried. He had an active social life but was never in the hunt to get married. His life had order and predictability and he wasn't in a hurry to make any major changes to it. He was in the men's league at the Enjoie Golf Club in Endicott and also played some of the other courses in the area. He had a regular foursome he played with. In the early spring, they would head to South Carolina to get a jump on the golf season and spend a few days playing golf and telling each other tall tales of golfing triumphs. One of the members of the foursome was Detective Todd Adams from the Binghamton Police Department. He was the best player in the group. Todd's level of play brought focus to the group as they had a standard to challenge. Todd's boss Lieutenant Hendricks, the chief of detectives, would also join the group when he could find the time. However, with two children in college, his time was always in demand. All of the men were involved in law enforcement, investigation or public prosecution which was a source of amusement to Lieutenant Hendrick's son Rhami. He called the group The Enforcers!

Alastair visited Emi's parents in Florida at least once a year. Now that his business had grown, some of his cases would take him outside New York and sometimes close to Florida. When this happened, he would take a few extra days and visit Nigel and Marie. They always remained close

Chapter 8

Alastair was in Friendsville, PA on a Thursday afternoon. He was meeting with a Binghamton attorney from Baker, Bright and Colson, the same firm where his sister Jane works. Friendsville is about ten miles south of Binghamton. They were in the process of taking on a case involving an accident at a bluestone quarry nearby. There's a large amount of bluestone rock in this part of Pennsylvania. Not a major industry but a new life for some of the farms as the quarries were usually on old farmland. At one of the quarries, there was a serious accident involving the use of dynamite. Five people were injured, two seriously. When the charges were set off, a major part of the quarry face blew out causing the injuries. Liability had not yet been established but clearly mistakes had been made. The injured parties were preparing to file a lawsuit. BBC as the law firm was known in town had retained Alastair to conduct an initial investigation so assess the overall situation and potential liability issues. If BBC represented the parties, they wanted to be on solid ground regarding liability. The quarry owner was adequately insured. The person who did the dynamiting, or blaster as he was called at the quarry, might not be insured. Lots to understand at this point.

After they finished the meeting, he was driving back to Endwell. PA 267 to NY 26 through Vestal Center and over the river to Endwell. He was still in Pennsylvania when Chantal called.

"Al, I got a call this afternoon from a lady who wants to meet with you tomorrow, later in the morning."

"Did she tell you it was about? I hope it's not marital surveillance. We don't do much of that anymore."

"No, she didn't want to go into any detail but this is something else. She mentioned a son who went missing some years back. She didn't say much more than that."

"Okay, try to set it up for eleven. I want to keep the afternoon open if I can."

"Golf?"

"Yeah, I've been running wide open for the past month. Sure would like to see how the other side lives. By the way, can you call Randy Martin and ask him to call me over the weekend. This quarry thing in Friendsville will be big and we need him to be part of the investigation. Five guys hurt, two seriously; I need to have him dig into their backgrounds. Also, can you find us a guy who knows dynamite and the topography around here. Let's all meet Monday morning."

Coming back from the quarry, Alastair turned off NY 26 north onto Glenwood Avenue in Vestal. He wanted to do a bit of shopping at the Weis Supermarket on the way home. It was a warm spring day with plenty of sunshine. When he pulled into the supermarket, he parked on the side of the lot under some trees bordering the parking lot to get out of the sun. It would help keep the car cool. It was next to a wooded area with a small stream designed to catch the runoff during heavy rains. He came out of the store about twenty minutes later with two bags of groceries. As he was loading them into the rear of his Nissan Murano, he heard a series of small barking sounds coming from the woods near his car. *Must be a dog chasing a critter,* he thought. But as he was getting into his SUV, he heard it again. Not so much a bark, more of a whimper. He looked into the wooded area but couldn't see anything so he walked in a bit. He heard more sounds and this time saw a dog. Broken right leg for sure and pretty banged up. The coat was all matted and filthy.

"What happened to you, my friend?" he said to the dog. "Who did this to you?"

Alastair had a quart of half and half and opened it up and poured some in a Starbucks coffee cup he still had in the car from an earlier stop. The dog wanted some but did not have the strength or mobility to take much. He poured it slowly into the dog's mouth with a bit more success.

"I need to get you to the vet. Come on, let's see if I can get you in the car. This will hurt but trust me, I'll be careful."

He opened the rear of the SUV and spread out a towel from his gym bag. The dog was in a lot of pain and as he moved the poor thing, there was a series of yelps and barks. However, no attempt to bite him. Maybe the dog understood? He took the dog to a clinic near his office. He had passed by the Veterinary Medical Center on Hooper Road in Endwell many times over the years. He didn't really know much about it but it had been there for as long as he'd been back. When he arrived, he asked the staff to be careful moving the dog as it was in a lot of pain and he was afraid of hurting it further. He waited in the lobby as the dog was being examined.

About forty-five minutes passed before the veterinarian came out and sat down beside Alastair. "Mr. Stewart, I'm Dr. Greg O'Day, I'm sorry I don't have any good news for you. You already know about the broken leg. There are significant internal injuries and broken ribs. This was not an accident, someone did this to her. I believe she was thrown from a moving car and it was not going slowly."

"I found her in the woods near the Weis market on Glenwood Avenue over in Vestal. I came straight here."

"May I be candid, sir? It may be best to just put her down. Her injuries are major. There's blood in her urine and in her mouth."

"Can you try to save her?"

"We can but I don't think there is much more than a twenty percent chance of her making it. Even if she does come through, there may be lingering problems. It won't be cheap to operate and if she doesn't make it, the money is lost."

"I want to try. I can't walk away from her."

"Alright, Mr. Stewart, I'll have to operate right away. Give me your phone number and I'll call you as soon as the surgery is finished. Prepare yourself for possible bad news. She may not survive the surgery. And if she does, she still may not make it."

About eight-thirty that night, Alastair got a call from Dr. O'Day. "She came through the surgery, Mr. Stewart. We found five broken ribs and internal bleeding along with the broken leg."

"Will she make it?"

"We won't know for a few days. There was a lot of infection. Come by here on Monday in the afternoon. If she dies tomorrow or over the weekend, I'll call you. No news is good news."

Thanks, Doctor, let's hope we talk on Monday and not before."

Chapter 9

"Al, your eleven o'clock appointment is here."

"Thanks, Chantal, just coming off this call, give me a minute and I'll come out to meet her."

A few minutes later, Alastair went to the reception area. Chantal's desk was near the center of the reception room. She was the agency receptionist, software trouble shooter, accountant, researcher, investigator and office manager. Actually, she did it all. She had two desks in the reception area. One for her computer and monitors she used for her research. It was located near the far wall of the room. The larger desk in the middle of the room was used to greet clients and answer the never-ending phone calls. Alastair could not imagine the office running without her. She had been with him for over eight years now on a full-time basis. Her husband and two children were part of his extended family.

"Mrs. Leonard, I'm Al Stewart, please come back to my office. Can I get you some coffee or water?"

"No, thank you."

"Give me just a second to grab a cup of coffee and we can get started."

"Well, if you're having one, I guess I will also. Cream, no sugar please,"

"Great, same way I take it. I hope you like it. It's a German specialty roast from Aldi."

When they went back to Alastair's office, Mrs. Leonard was a bit nervous. Alastair noticed she was continuing to stir her coffee and was seated on the edge of her chair. Alastair had a large well-furnished office. In one corner he had three large armchairs surrounding a coffee table. He found it was more comfortable for his clients as opposed to talking to them over his desk. Off to the side, he had a separate workstation for his computer, two large monitors and two low file cabinets with combination locks for the office files. The walls had some signed prints by an English artist he collected, L.S. Lowry. The best ones were at his house, but the three on the office walls were quite good. He loved the simplicity of the artist's work and yet the strong message it provided. His office floor was hardwood and had a large oriental rug. He often thought, *not your average PI's office, that's for sure!* He wanted to have a professional presentation. Next to the reception area were two small conference rooms also well appointed. His sister Jane had been the decorating consultant.

"Mrs. Leonard, I'm guessing you've never met with a private investigator before, so let me provide some information about how I operate. I'm licensed by the state of New York. Just like an attorney or priest, all information provided to me is held in strictest confidence. If I feel I need to release some of your case information to help in an investigation, I'll obtain your permission first. If I feel I cannot help you, I'll let you know up front and not charge for unnecessary work."

"Thank you, Mr. Stewart. I appreciate your candor. Please call me Marilyn."

"Okay, and I'm Al. It's actually Alastair but I go by Al. Tell me how I can help you."

"I want you to find my son Raymond."

"He's missing?"

"Yes, almost ten years now,"

"I assume the police were called in and there was an active investigation."

"They were called and candidly, worked very hard, but they were never able to find him."

"Why do you want me to look for him now? Do you have new information or evidence?"

"I wish I did but it's about me now. I am a breast cancer survivor. Recently, I found out that the cancer was back after seven years. I'm scared and don't know if this is the final chapter for me. My doctor says I have a very manageable condition but I'm so worried that I'll die without at least trying once more to find Raymond. He has autism and I'm always worried that he cannot look after himself. He needs support."

"You never had any contact or additional information over the years?"

"No, nothing. He disappeared one night and I've never heard from him in all these years. My heart tells me he's still alive but this may just be the hopes of an old lady."

"Marilyn, I don't want to mislead you but given all these years, the odds are pretty slim that he's still alive. This is hard to say but I don't want to raise any false hopes."

"I understand, Hubert my husband and I have discussed this at length. We're prepared for that outcome."

"Who was the lead investigator on the case?"

"It was Detective Runnings at the Binghamton Police Department. He's been retired now for a couple of years. Before he retired, he called me and told me he was sorry for not being able to close the case. He said he always kept it open and hoped that something would turn up. It was so thoughtful of him."

"I knew Bill when he was with the police. I first met him through a mutual friend when I was back here visiting my sister. I was with the FBI in those days. When I set up the office here, our paths crossed a few times. He was a good cop. I'm sure someone has the case now. I'll call

Lieutenant Elton Hendricks; he's chief of detectives and check in with him."

"Thank you. It's comforting to know there's someone looking at this again."

"We need to look at this in stages. If I have a way forward, we'll take the next steps. If I can't see a way forward, I'll stop the investigation. This can get very expensive quickly. I don't want to take your money without being confident we are making progress. We'll do some initial research using our office resources. I'll also meet with Lieutenant Hendricks and Detective Runnings. I want to understand what they found in their investigation. The initial charge will be for around twenty hours of work. I charge $300 an hour for this stage. That will mean a cost of $6000. I'll send you an itemized invoice when we finish. So, based on our initial look; If we think there is something worth following up, we'll make a decision on the next step. I won't be able to start our research on this until later next week. We have some open cases that we're finishing up and Chantal our office manager will be tied up until then."

"That's fine. Thank you for being so candid with me."

"I'll make some calls to the police this week and set up a meeting."

Chapter 10

Alastair called Lieutenant Hendricks.

"Elton, it's Al Stewart. How's your golf game?"

The two men knew each other from playing in the men's league at the Enjoie Golf course in Endicott. Both played at the same level and happily shared their adventures or maybe misadventures!

"I think the course record is safe for another year," laughed the lieutenant.

"Same from my side, but I'm satisfied with my game these past months. If I could get to the high eighties or low nineties and stay there I'd be a happy camper."

"Take me with you, Al!"

"Do you remember a kid who went missing about ten years ago or so. Name is Raymond Leonard. I think Bill Runnings was the lead investigator."

"I do remember the case but not in much detail now. You're right, Bill was the lead. He retired a few years ago. I know he's still around; you want to talk with him?"

"I do and would also like to take a look at the case file. His mother was in to see me and wants to try one more time to find him. She doesn't have an issue with the police work and in fact was very complimentary about Bill. She has a potential life ending diagnosis and wants to try again to find her son."

"Wow, poor lady. Carrying that grief for all these years. Why don't you call Bill and see what he can tell you? The two of you can come to the station and look over what we have on file. Talk to Bill first, I think it'll help in the review of the files."

"I'll do that and get back to you. In the meantime, fix your golf swing. Close your eyes and swing hard!"

"Man, why didn't I think of that," laughed the lieutenant!

Next up was Bill Runnings. Sometimes retired cops are reluctant to talk about their unsolved cases. Maybe they just don't like to give out information or just feel embarrassed about not solving the case. Alastair could probably get the case information under the freedom of information act but this is sometimes a long process, and the file could be redacted to limit information considered confidential or sensitive. Alastair's and Bill's path had crossed a few times over the years and each man respected the other's role. Within the police department, Alastair had a good reputation. He cooperated with the police and shared information. He was hopeful that Bill would be in a sharing mood.

"Bill, this is Al Stewart, is this a good time to talk?"

"Now that I'm retired, anytime is a good time to talk. What's the good word from Endwell Investigations?"

"Remember Mrs. Leonard, Raymond Leonard's mother? He was a lad who went missing some years back. She came by earlier in the week. She wants to take another look at her son's case. She's worried she has a terminal diagnosis and wanted to try one more time to find her son. Bill, she has no issues with you or the Binghamton Police. She had really nice things to say about you and the other cops."

"I wish we could have closed the case Al. It's one of about five I sort of have taken home with me. How can I help you?"

"Can we meet and talk about the case and then go to headquarters and you walk me through the case file?"

"Sure, I have a couple of notebooks at home about the case that are outside the standard case file entries. I've kept them with me. I'll bring them along. Let's meet at your office. Best have a quiet place to talk. What time works for you?"

"Next Monday around nine? I'll have coffee ready for you."

"Don't forget the donuts. Old cop habits die hard!"

The following Monday, Alastair arrived at the office around eight. He had a full day ahead of him and needed to get a running start. About ten minutes after he arrived, there was a notification on his mobile that he had a text message. He saw that it was from Dr. O'Day at the veterinary hospital. Oh, shit, he thought, the poor dog must have died over the weekend. Reluctantly, he opened the message. *"Mr. Stewart, the dog had a good weekend. She's much better! Quite a surprise. Just wanted to let you know."*

This is great. What a great start to the week! thought Alastair, *Guess I've got a family now. Wish I could go right over there but I've got Bill Runnings here at nine.*

When Bill arrived, they settled into a small conference room next to the reception area. Alastair asked Chantal to join the meeting. He anticipated a lot of research if they went forward with the case and wanted Chantal to be involved from the beginning. Bill had a fair amount of case information with him in two spiral notebooks full of his notes. The notebooks covered ten years.

"Where do you want to start, Al?"

"Why don't you talk me through the case so I can get a feeling for it. We can dig into the files after that. I'm more interested in your perspective on this. You've got the most experience. I'm a bit skeptical if anything can be done; It's been so long."

"I've felt that way for a few years now. You know the game. Once the clock starts running, time is not on your side. The one thing that always stayed with me is the fact that he's autistic. I checked with The Sheltered Workshop where he worked about how self-sufficient he was and if he could survive by himself. He was twenty-three at the time and I thought he might have life skills to make it alone. They didn't think so. He had developed good social skills to the point where he could interact with other folks but that was not enough."

"Were you thinking that he just ran away or got hopelessly lost?"

"Not really. I always thought he got picked up, taken for a ride, robbed and killed. Then was dumped in the woods. Easy to dispose of a body in the country around here. Whatever happened to him, somebody else was involved. He couldn't have just wandered off and disappeared."

"Did you ever get any tips or anonymous calls?"

"Nothing, not one tip. We questioned a lot of the guys we arrested back then. We were always looking for information. We had the usual actors trying to leverage their charges and jail time with anything they thought we'd believe. We ran them all down but no joy. The guy disappeared and we never heard another thing."

"Do you have his fingerprints and DNA?"

"We got his prints and DNA from The Sheltered Workshop. It was part of their protocol in working with disabled folks. We matched it with prints from his parent's home where he lived. We also got some DNA from his hairbrush. Never got a hit on either of them. I always kept the file open and would look at it periodically. Always hoping to see something I missed. When I retired, my partner Todd Adams took over the case."

Chantal joined the conversation. "Al, let me do some research on this before you guys look at the case files at police headquarters. It may help with your review. I'd like to get a feeling for what else was happening around that time."

Bill responded, "It was a busy time back then. On the same day or within a day, there was a double homicide in a lot over on the west side. Looked like a drug deal gone bad or someone stealing a dealer's stash. That case was also never closed."

"Do you think they were connected?" ask Chantal.

"We looked closely at it but couldn't connect them."

"Was Raymond using?"

"No, I don't think he even knew what drugs were and if he did, how to buy the stuff. He lived a simple life, well structured. He stayed in his orbit so to speak. That worked for him and provided stability."

"I wonder if there was a connection? Two significant events. I don't like coincidences," said Alastair.

Chapter 11

After the meeting, Alastair quickly drove over to the Veterinary Medical Center on Hooper Road. When he arrived, Doctor O'Day was just coming out of the surgery room, still in his scrubs. When he saw Alastair, he broke into a big smile.

"I would have bet a paycheck against this, but here we are! She came through in great shape. I think she's well on her way to a pretty full recovery."

"When can I take her home?"

"She'll have to be with us for another two weeks or so. We board animals here and can keep her with us. The cages are large and the techs can take her outside and exercise her when she's a bit further along. For now, just rest and whatever she wants to eat. I have her on a course of antibiotics that will finish in ten days. After that we can take the next steps."

"Can I see her?"

"Oh, yes, and please come by anytime while she's here. It will help in the recovery. By the way, does the dog have a name?"

"No. This has all happened so fast, I've not thought about it at all. She didn't have a collar or tag when I found her."

"Well, the assistants have been calling her Sherlock. They picked it up from your line of work."

"Sherlock? Hmm, why not, I sort of like it. Sherlock is a man's name. Do you think she'll mind?"

"I'll ask her," laughed the doctor.

When Alastair went back to see the dog, AKA Sherlock now, she was sleeping on her side with a large cast on the broken leg. Her cage was on an examination table. Alastair pulled up a chair next to the table and sat quietly looking at the dog. He opened the cage and gently patted Sherlock. She opened her eyes and recognized him. She moved her head closer to his hand and let out a small whimper type of sound. Doctor O'Day came back into the room to check Sherlock's temperature.

"Nice and stable, Al, just what we want now. The antibiotics are working well."

"By the way, what kind of dog is she?"

"She looks to be a blend of pure Husky and German Sheppard. Maybe two years old. Beautiful dog, even in her present condition. She knows you now and has bonded with you. You've got a soulmate, my friend."

"I'm so happy, Doctor, this is a real gift. It's just me in the house and now I'll have a roommate! Rest well, Sherlock, I'll be back tomorrow."

When Alastair got back to the office, Randy Martin was already there. He was sort of an odd-job guy for the agency. Part time investigator and researcher. He was a great tech head, always up to speed on the latest equipment. He did a lot of the surveillance work for the agency. Alastair wanted him to join the firm on a full-time basis but he was too much of a free spirit. He made a living by providing technical services around town. But he was always available for Endwell Investigations when needed, so *take the money and run* thought Alastair. He was lucky to have found him. Actually, it was Randy who found him. He had come to the office about six years ago. He was like a bear with a sore paw. Not a happy guy.

"My neighbor is committing insurance fraud! He was in a fender bender and is trying to milk the claim as a major accident. He has a neck brace and walker and it's all for show. I see him in the backyard working in his garden and on his back deck without any of that stuff. It really pisses me off. I need someone with some horsepower to straighten him out."

Alastair agreed to take a look at it but didn't have to do much as Randy had all the evidence in hand. Pictures and video. The neighbor was represented by a local attorney who had a less than stellar reputation with the Broome County Bar Association. Alastair set up a meeting with the attorney and his "suffering client." After showing them the evidence, he suggested that they may want to drop their case or he would send the evidence to the bar association, police, and insurance company. Having seen the light, the case was immediately dropped. He never charged Randy for the service even after repeated requests. He always said he would get around to it.

Alastair recognized Randy's technical and investigative skills and from there the relationship grew. Chantal always thought of them as the odd couple. Alastair always organized and on top of the problem, and Randy coming into the middle of it and going in both directions. The two of them made a good team.

It wasn't clear how the case regarding the quarry accident would move forward. There were a lot of issues to be understood. They knew the wall on the face of the quarry blew out and collapsed after being dynamited but that was about all at this point. Negligence was not clearly established. Five people were hurt, two of them seriously. The law firm was very interested in the case but a lot of work needed to be done ahead of filing any lawsuits. They suspected negligence on the part of the explosives manufacturer or blaster at this point but all the evidence had yet to be gathered and analyzed. Maybe both the quarry owner or blaster had not properly assessed the topography of the surrounding land and it wasn't safe to blast? Lots of unanswered questions.

Alastair's agency had been contracted by Baker, Bright & Colson to perform an initial assessment and gather the data. He would be paid for his time whether or not the law firm decided to take the case. Alastair would have to call in outside experts to assess the explosives used and condition of the quarry. If a suit went forward and BB&C prevailed, he would also participate in the settlement. This was a big case for Endwell Investigations. Alastair was excited about its scope and complexity. *I may need to find a dynamite guy who does this kind of work and certainly somebody who knows about the land around here and at the quarries. If this does go forward, we need to be on firm ground.* No pun intended!

Chapter 12

After they finished their meeting on the quarry accident, Alastair and Randy sat in his office finishing off some stale coffee and talking about Raymond Leonard. Randy was not fully read into the case, so Alastair took the time to bring him up to speed.

"Randy, I'm convinced Bill Runnings was right in his assessment that Raymond could not have survived alone. He wasn't capable. Somebody played a role in his disappearance. The double homicide on the west side at the same time is something we need to understand."

"Do you think they're connected?"

"Yeah, I do, but have no idea how. I just have a gut feeling that they're tied together. I've never been a strong believer in coincidences. I'm going to meet with Bill Runnings at the police station day after tomorrow. We're going to review the Leonard case files. I also want to take a look at the double homicide. I'm going to call Raymond's mother tomorrow and try to dig a bit deeper into her memory of the events."

"Looks like you have a lot of balls in the air, Al."

"I sure do. On top of that, the time since the disappearance is troubling. You know how leads and information dry up over time; we're dealing with that also."

The next day Alastair called Raymond's mother.

"Marilyn, got time for some questions?"

"Always, what can I tell you?"

"How did Raymond spend his time? I know we discussed this earlier, but I'd like to try and dig a bit deeper."

"Well, he worked at The Sheltered Workshop during the week. A van would come by and take him to work and bring him home. He helped Hubert out around the house doing odd jobs and also managed the accounts for the house. He was very good in this area. He had a good head for numbers. He also did most of the grocery shopping for us."

"How did he get to the stores?"

"He walked. There's a Weis supermarket about five or so blocks from the house. He walked there. He had a backpack and shopping cart. He could handle most of the groceries. We made up for any shortfalls with a car trip on the weekends if needed. He was pretty much out in all kinds of weather. He liked the challenge and called them adventures."

"What time did he usually go to the store?"

"Mostly, when he got home from work. Sometimes on the weekends but mostly during the week in the evening."

"Did you worry about him getting lost?"

"Not really, Raymond and I had been doing these walks since he was a little guy. As he got older, he went by himself, we wanted to encourage his independence. At some point, we wouldn't be able to look after him and Hubert and I wanted him to be as independent as his abilities would allow."

"Tell me again about the night he went missing."

"There isn't a lot to tell. He came home from work around five o'clock as usual and went out to the grocery store after dinner, around six-thirty. It was a nice night and he wanted to get out for a bit, and we needed some things from the store. He left the house and that was the last we saw of him. I called the police about eight that night to report him missing. I told them he was disabled so they started a missing persons search right away."

"Did he have his shopping cart and backpack with him?"

"Yes, he never went to the store without them. I have a picture of him with the shopping cart and backpack. I think we took it a few months before he went missing."

"Good, we may need it at some point. Do you remember what he was wearing the night he disappeared?"

"I think so. I know we gave the police a description of the clothes when we first reported him missing."

"I'm sure you did but sometimes a missing detail is remembered and it can be very helpful."

"He had on a green windbreaker. Sort of a dark grass color; nylon fabric."

"Did it have any logos?"

"No, Raymond didn't like anything like that on his clothes. He had a baseball cap also; Dark blue, no markings. Dungarees and low-cut sneakers."

"Did he have a mobile phone?"

"He had one but didn't use it very much. He didn't carry it with him all the time. I was always finding it around the house and kept reminding him to keep it with him. He was comfortable with the phone technology but was not interested in keeping it with him."

"Did he have his phone with him the night he went missing?"

"No, it's still here. It's in his room. Do you want to come over and take a look around his room? I've not changed much since he went missing."

"Maybe later, but for now I think our concentration needs to be with the police files and Bill Runnings."

"Please say hello to Detective Runnings for me. I remember his dedication and hard work trying to find Raymond."

"I'll call you after my meeting. Maybe something will come from the meeting that we can build on. If we can't move forward, we need to have a candid conversation about the next steps. I don't want to waste your money on a fruitless search."

"I understand. It's been so long now I have no illusions. I'm prepared for the worst."

"Don't give up yet," replied Alastair.

Chapter 13

When Alister arrived at the police station about eight-thirty, Bill was already there. He was in Lieutenant Elton Hendricks office.

"Al, come on in," said the lieutenant, "it's been a while. We need to get out on the golf course soon. I bought a new putter and it's really made a difference."

"Sure, get your son Rhami to join us. We need some talent in the group!"

"The kid has really made progress. I think he'll try out for the college golf team. He loves the game and is really happy when we're on the course. He can get in the zone and really focus."

"Bill, don't you want to join this talented group?" asked Lieutenant Hendricks.

"Not me. I tried it once and couldn't hit the ball."

"So what!" laughed Alastair, "We do that all the time!"

"Bill has all the files on Raymond Leonard in the conference room," said the lieutenant, "I'll leave you with Bill. Let me know what you think after you finish."

"I'd also like to look at the case files for that double homicide that happened about the same time. I keep thinking that there is some connection but it's only a hunch at this time."

"We did also but were never able to connect them," said Bill, "I know Raymond was not into drugs, but we thought he might have stumbled onto something. But I would have expected him to be killed at the scene if he saw anything. Those guys don't mess around; they don't take prisoners."

Maybe he was able to run away?" said Alastair.

Alastair and Bill spent most of the morning reviewing Raymond's case file and Bill's notes which were actually more comprehensive than the standard files kept by the police. Bill's attention to details was evident. Alastair was particularly interested in the scope of the search for Raymond. The Binghamton Police had used the media extensively, both television and the newspapers. Pictures had also been circulated across the state to the media and law enforcement. Raymond's case remained on their open case review for five years. On top of that, Bill Runnings never forgot or gave up the investigation. But in the end, no joy.

"Bill, I don't know what else could have been done. I don't think I'd have done anything different. All the bases were covered."

"I tell myself that," said Bill, "but in the end, we didn't find him and that's all that matters. Let's look at the double homicide. Lieutenant Hendricks and Todd Adams handled it. I'll get Todd to join us with the files."

Alastair also knew Todd from the Enjoie Golf Course and their trips to South Carolina in the early spring. He was one of the better players in the men's league. *Seems like all of them are better players,* thought Alastair, *such is life in the heady game of golf. Hmm, maybe I should steal Elton's new putter and reinvent myself! Maybe not. I can't buy or steal my way out of my game!* Todd came in with four large folders.

"Let me walk you through this before we look at the files. Two gentlemen, one from this area, were killed in a drug deal gone bad. We don't know if it was one or two guys who did the killing but whoever fired the shots knew what he was doing. Both were shot in the chest and then in the head to make sure. A double tap as the hitmen call it. Typical professional hit. No drugs or shell casings were found at the crime scene. The bullets we were able to recover from the bodies were thirty-eight caliber. They were not in the system. Sort of an odd choice of gun as most of the drug guys use Glocks, and some of the hitmen prefer a twenty-two caliber as their weapon of choice. We're guessing it was a revolver as no shell casings were found. The head shots were messy. We didn't recover any bullets from them. They were pretty well damaged by their skulls. We don't know if they were killed as part of a robbery or a drug deal gone bad. Whoever killed them took the drugs."

"Who were the guys killed?"

"One was local and the other from Monticello down in the Catskills. Most likely the drugs came from there or the city. Probably going to be moved further around the state from Binghamton. We had rap sheets on both guys. They were not big players but had been around the business for some time."

Alastair asked, "What are your thoughts about the shooting?"

"We think it was someone trying to send a message to these guys about territory and who owns what turf. They may have been trying to expand their territory. After they were whacked, the drug business around here changed. New faces and new problems. It's likely that some new guys were moving in; we just don't know."

"Did you ever get close to the shooter?"

"No. We think it was a pro from the city. Usually, the foot soldiers shoot up the place with automatic pistols. Always sloppy work. Whoever shot these guys was probably working a contract. We were never able to put a face or MO with the shooter. As I mentioned earlier the weapon of choice for the shooting was odd. A thirty-eight-caliber pistol is usually not used in a hit. We checked around but couldn't find a hitman who favored the thirty-eight. We kept the case open for quite a while but then it went cold. We needed to chase other bad boys."

The detectives reviewed the case files. They were well organized but didn't add much more to Todd's narrative. As they were finishing the review of the files, Todd pulled out a series of photos of the crime scene.

The pictures of the bodies showed considerable head damage. Clearly shot at a close range. As they were looking at the crime scene photos, Alastair focused on a series of photos of the lot and surrounding area. In one of the photos, he noticed a shopping cart off to the side of the lot. It was on its side at the entrance to the lot just off the sidewalk. The vacant lot had a fair amount of trash which had accumulated over the past few years. But the shopping cart was not like the other trash. It was not weathered or broken. It had been left there recently.

"Can you make me a copy of these two photos?"

Todd replied, "You can take them. Bring them back when you're finished."

"What are you thinking?" asked Bill.

"Raymond had a shopping cart. He took it with him everywhere. I want to show these pictures to his mother."

When Alastair got home that evening, he called Raymond's mother.

"Marilyn, can I come over in the morning? I want to show you some pictures."

"I'm here all morning. I have a chemo treatment in the afternoon, though."

"Morning is fine. Can we meet at nine?"

"I'll be ready."

The next day Alastair was at Marilyn's along with Randy and the photos. He wanted Randy to be with him as another set of ears and eyes. Randy often saw things others missed in a conversation. From there they would be going to the stone quarry so it saved time running back to the office. Marilyn was clearly nervous when the two men arrived. Alastair quickly sensed her fear and put it to rest.

"Marilyn, please don't worry. I am not going to show you photos of bodies or anything like that. I want you to take a look at two pictures and tell me what you see."

When he showed her the photos, there was a quick intake of breath. She put her hand to her mouth and whispered something that neither man could hear. It might have been a prayer.

"That's Raymond's shopping cart!"

"How do you know?"

"Look at the handle. See those two hooks? Raymond put them there so he could hang a light bag from them when the cart was full. Here, look at the picture I showed you earlier. The one we took of him with his cart. See, there're the hooks! Where were these pictures taken?"

Randy answered, "In a lot about six blocks from your house. It's been cleaned up and Habitat for Humanity built two houses there."

"I know where that is and it's on the way to the Weis Supermarket. Raymond must have walked past it."

"Most likely he did," said Alastair, "but that's all we know at this point. He was there."

"Will you keep on looking?"

"I think we should. We need to find out more about the drug operation. Marilyn, don't get your hopes up too high. We don't know anything more than he was there."

Alastair called Bill Runnings to let him know about the shopping cart.

"Can you give Todd a call and let him know; I think we need to meet again and dig a bit deeper into this. The shooter could have grabbed him and taken him somewhere, killed him and dumped him."

"Damn," said Bill, "I never saw the grocery cart. Just saw junk in the lot."

"I never would have spotted it if Marilyn hadn't shown me a picture of Raymond with the cart the day before we met. We got lucky."

"Nice hit, Al, we've got a new direction now."

Chapter 14

From Marilyn's house the two men headed south to Pennsylvania to the bluestone quarry. When Alastair first got involved in the blasting accident investigation, he didn't know much about the bluestone quarries in northern Pennsylvania. He expected them to look like marble quarries. Large deep open pits. This was not the case with these quarries. Mostly, they were part of a farm probably not in operation anymore. This one near Friendsville was part of a farm. The quarry was on the side of a hill. A large part of the hill was exposed indicating it had been in operation for some time.

The scene of the accident was easy to spot. One side of the face of the quarry was not uniform and had a lot of debris at the base. The quarry face had not collapsed but clearly had been damaged by the dynamite blast. Both men stood there looking the quarry face and trying to understand what they were looking at.

"I found a guy at the University of Scranton who may be able to help us. He's a physics professor and geology is his hobby. He's local and knows the area," said Randy.

"How'd you find him?"

"I did a surveillance job for a guy in town a few months ago. I ran into him last week and was talking about the accident. It was still in the news. He said he'd heard about it from his brother at the university. I told him we were looking for a geologist to help out in the investigation. He gave me his number."

"Good stuff. Give him a call and let's talk with him."

As they were talking, Teddy Bellmore the owner of the farm came over.

"You're the investigator from the law firm in Binghamton, you were here before."

"That's me and this is Randy, my associate. We want to look around, get a feel for the quarry and surrounding area. Is that okay with you?"

"I guess. I've retained a lawyer from over in Montrose. I don't know where this is headed so I want to have proper representation. If there's any follow-up between us, I want it to be coordinated through his office."

"That's a good way to go. We'll respect your wishes. I'm going to have a geologist take a look at the quarry. I'll work through your attorney to set up a date and time."

"Okay. Off the record, Mr. Stewart, I don't understand this myself yet. We've been working two quarry sites on my farm for almost twenty years. We've never had a problem. The bluestone on the farm is solid. Large masses of it. That's what makes this quarry special. You can quarry large pieces. I've been working with the same blaster, Travis Durgan, for over ten years. He was trained in the Army. Knows his stuff and only works around in this area of the state. This was not just a careless accident. There was something going on that doesn't fit."

"Were your guys standing too close to the blast site?"

"No, not at all. Travis, the blasting guy, is very cautious and always makes sure the site is secure before he sets anything off. He's been working on this quarry for a number of years and knows the terrain. When he finishes a job, he always checks the blast site to make sure it's stable before he lets the guys back on the quarry face. I trust him."

"Thanks for the comments."

Two week later, Professor McGinn from the University of Scranton met with Randy at the accident site. Randy had Sherlock with him. The dog loved the outings and was always eager to get into the car for the next adventure. As the two men talked, Sherlock bounded over the nearby fields chasing all the critters. Catching them was not the plan, just run around with them. The dog's recovery was complete. She was in a safe place now and thriving. She spent most of her day at the office with Alastair and Chantal. First one to greet the clients with a wagging tail and loud woof! Everyone loved the dog; Randy called her the office ambassador!

Randy and Alastair expected that Professor McGinn would find some issue with the land that would explain the collapse of the quarry wall. But that was not the case. The professor spent a considerable amount of time walking around the quarry site, both at the top and bottom. He was particularly interested in the debris field. A lot of the debris was in smaller pieces.

"I'm not an explosives expert but from the size of the individual pieces, I think something pretty powerful went off. Lots of small pieces. Interesting."

"What about the land around the quarry?" asked Randy.

"I don't see anything from the land that would explain the collapse. It's high and dry here and the surrounding area is pretty much solid rock. Not good for farming, that's for sure. I'd guess the Bellmore's were dairy farmers. If you want to dig a bit deeper, no pun intended, we could do some drilling and take core samples but candidly, the reason for the collapse lies somewhere else. I think the problem is with the explosive equipment or placement of the blasting holes. The ground here is stable."

"Okay, I'll tell Al about your findings. Can we come back to you if he thinks we need to look further?"

"Sure, just call my office. I'm on campus most days."

Randy and Sherlock headed back to Endwell Investigations. A nice ride from Friendsville. *I love the county roads,* thought Randy, *light traffic and lots of great scenery.* Sherlock was sitting up front in the passenger seat, enjoying the ride. When they got back to the office, Chantal and Alastair were in a meeting about a new client and talking about the research that would be required for the investigation. He heard his name come up a couple of times during their conversation about the new case. Apparently the issue involved a house fire. The fire department had found an accelerant and although not conclusive, they had serious doubts about the cause of the fire. The insurance on the house was over four hundred thousand dollars which got the attention of the insurance company. *Hmm, this could be interesting,* thought Randy.

When Alastair and Chantal finished, Randy was waiting for him in the reception area. Sherlock had settled in for a nap after the busy time with the critters in Friendsville.

"How'd it go?"

"The professor doesn't think the land had anything to do with the collapse of the quarry face. He said he could drill some core samples to make sure but in his opinion, it would be a waste of money."

"You know, we're at the point where Baker, Bright and Colson need to make up their minds if they want to take the case. They'll need to bring a suit against someone. Either the quarry owner, blaster, or whoever. I want to talk to the blaster but without a subpoena, I doubt he'll want to talk with me. Why would he? We're trying to build a case and it could be against him! We need access to the quarry owner, blaster and dynamite company to get to the bottom of this. I don't think any of them will talk to us without a subpoena."

"What are you going to do?"

"I want to speak to Professor McGinn and find out more about his thinking on the cause of the accident. He's neutral and I'd like to understand this better. I'll call him tomorrow."

When Alastair called the professor the next day, he caught him on the way to a class. They agreed to speak at two o'clock in the afternoon.

That afternoon, the two men connected on a Zoom call. They had not met yet and Alastair thought a Zoom call would be a good way to meet for the first time.

"Where is that great dog of yours?" asked the professor.

"Sherlock is out with Randy again. She never lets him out of her sight. When she see him heading for the door, she's right after him. I think she's our canine detective."

"Take good care of her, she's special."

"That she is, sir, I'm a lucky guy. Professor, I know you don't have a lot of factual evidence at this point, so I don't want to put you in an awkward position. I'm interested in your opinion. Candidly, the law firm I'm working for will have to make a decision about whether to represent the injured parties in a lawsuit and more importantly, whom to sue. We're comfortable that there was negligence but not sure where it lies."

"I guess you don't want to sue all the parties, that would be a bit complicated and I wonder if it's legal. If you sued all the parties, it would look like a fishing expedition! In my opinion, Mr. Stewart, there's nothing wrong with the land. The ground is stable and I don't think it played a role in the cause of the accident. If you want that in a deposition, I would have to drill core samples to back up my hypothesis."

"That leaves the dynamite company and the blaster then," replied Alastair.

"That's about it. I can't tell if the dynamite was defective or the blaster was negligent but I'm comfortable in my position that the land was not a factor."

"This is very helpful, thank you. I'll get with the lawyers and let them make the call on the next steps. If the case goes forward, they may well want to depose you."

Certainly, just make sure they understand that for me to state under oath that the land was not a factor, I'll need to drill core samples."

"I'll pass it on, thanks so much for your time."

"My pleasure, take good care of your dog!"

"Always; good day sir."

When he finished the call with Professor McGinn, he called Baker, Bright & Colson. He spoke to the lead attorney on the case, Henry McArdle.

"Henry, based on a preliminary look at this, I don't think the quarry itself is in play. I had a physics professor from the University of Scranton take a look at it. He's not a geologist by trade but clearly knows his stuff. He'll provide a deposition if requested but will want to drill some core samples first to support his position. I think liability rests with either the blaster or the explosives company."

"Interesting, let me talk to the business committee. We'll be meeting tomorrow. I think we'll run with this one. What do you need from us at this point?"

"I've probably taken this as far as I can for now. We'll need to interview the blaster and explosives company under oath. They won't talk to me without a subpoena. I have my investigator Randy and office manager doing some background checks on the both of them. I want to get a bit closer to this before we depose them."

"No problem, we'll cover you."

The next call was to Chantal. She was over at Binghamton University doing some research on fire accelerants for their new case. Now that they had been retained by the insurance company, the cause of spread of the fire needed to be understood. They had the fire department report but they needed more detail. It did mention accelerants but was not specific. Chantal didn't think it was the usual culprit gasoline. If so the fire department report would have mentioned it. Something else was going on here. Although not currently employed as an engineer, the owner of the house had a degree in chemical engineering which got Chantal's attention. The case had an odor to it as Alastair liked to say.

"Chantal, can you get hold of Randy and look into the blaster and explosives company who were involved in the quarry accident in Friendsville? You don't need to contact either party, just see what information and background you can find on them. Were they involved in any other accidents, lawsuits or performance issues in the past? Confirm that the blaster is licensed and insured. Same for the explosives company. If either one of them was in trouble in the past, we need to know about it."

"Okay. By the way, one of the kids in my neighborhood is a student here. I gave her a ride over to pick up some books. Sherlock is with us and is now the star attraction at the Student Union. They may try to elect her president of the union! I won't be finished here until after six, so I'll take Sherlock home with me. My kids will be thrilled to have her over."

"Sure, how come everyone loves Sherlock and nobody loves me?"

"Do you want the long or the short answer to that, Al!"

"Best, leave it alone I think!"

Chapter 15

The next day, Alastair had a call from Bill Runnings waiting for him when he arrived at the office. He was always a bit early. He liked to have the coffee ready when Chantal arrived. Like Alastair, she was fussy about her coffee. Both the brand and strength. Aldi's special German blend answered the mail for them. Chantal liked the fat-free half and half from Price Shopper and always made sure there was a good supply in the fridge. Always start the day with a good cup of coffee! Randy and Chantal were busy doing background checks on the blaster and explosives company, so there wasn't much for him to do until they finished and the law firm filed a suit. Maybe two weeks or so.

Coffee in hand, he called Bill Runnings back. He answered on the second ring.

"You're up and running early, what's up?"

"Old cop habits, I guess. I still wake up early. I spoke with Todd about Raymond's shopping cart being at the drug murder crime scene. He'd like for us to meet again. What's your schedule look like?"

"I'm pretty open. We're doing some background checks on a pending case so I'm pretty much available. How about tomorrow? I need to sort out an upcoming case today."

"Let's meet at Todd's office at nine tomorrow. If that's not good for him, I'll call you back. No news is good news."

The next day, the three men met in the conference room next to Lieutenant Hendrick's office. Todd had his computer plugged into the overhead projector to make it easier for them to see the data. He had some ideas and was eager to share them with Bill and Alastair.

"Al, when you linked the shopping cart to the drug crime scene, it really got me thinking."

"Always dangerous for a cop!" laughed Bill.

"I know, Bill, I try to avoid it if I can!" responded Todd to a round of laughs.

The men settled into a review of the case, yet again. The challenge was still to find out what happened to Raymond. They now knew he was at the scene but nothing more. Rather than speculate, they decided to go back to the very beginning and concentrate on the drug trade in upstate New York. The murders in Binghamton were over ten years ago and a lot had changed in the drug business. There was a lot more dope on the streets and from many sources. Now the market was fragmented with methamphetamine or meth as it is known on the street and being made in garages and kitchens all over the place. However, back in the day, as we all like to say, the drug trade in upstate New York was essentially supplied from New York and New Jersey. Sourced out of the city and distributed by mules making trips from the city or upstate distribution points.

"We need to focus on how the game was played ten plus years ago and not how it's done today. It's another world now."

Bill said, "Binghamton was not a major distribution point back then. Albany was a bigger play, and maybe Syracuse. But there was a loop from Binghamton west to Elmira and Corning and up to Rochester. I think Batavia may also have been in the loop."

"Why Binghamton?" asked Alastair.

Todd replied, "It's usually based on personal connections. Family, friends, whatever clicks. They run it for a bit and then it collapses because of a gang war, or someone gets caught. Always a very fluid structure. But back then I know that loop existed. I was a street cop and we busted a number of local dealers. They all were getting their dope from the city. Elmira and Rochester were mentioned as destinations for the drugs from the city. The guys we busted were always trying to cut a deal by throwing us a bone or two. Drug sentences back then were really stiff so they tried to walk them back if they could."

"I remember those days well," said Bill, "most of our action was from the streets. We never got very close to any of the big players. The guys we busted were afraid of giving us too much or they would be killed by the dealers."

"What about the Binghamton guy who was killed in the lot?" asked Alastair.

Bill replied, "He was part of a local group, maybe four or five guys. They were early players in the drug trade here. We busted them all at one time or other. They were small time dealers. Most of their customers gave them up in a heartbeat."

Alastair asked, "Are any of these stellar citizens still around?"

"That's what I was wondering about also," said Todd, "of the four that we know about, two are dead. Looking at the last two, we can't find one, but the other is still with us and in the Broome County Jail!"

"You're kidding! What's the charge? Bet it was jaywalking!" laughed Bill.

"Traffic stop for speeding. He got really mad and took a swing at the cop. Said he was not speeding and was being framed. As you might imagine our boy was drunk. We didn't find any drugs but tossed him in jail as he hit the cop and knocked him down. Right now, we're letting him stew for a bit and will charge him this week." replied Todd, "I think we should talk with him. He certainly knows the history and if his information is good, we may consider cutting him some slack on the pending charge. I don't want to give him a get out of jail free card, he assaulted a cop after all. If it looks like he can help us, I'll talk to the cop he hit to let him know where we're headed. The cops working the streets are always the last ones to know about changes in the charges."

"I remember those days," said Bill.

"I'll set up the meeting with Mr. John J. Maloney, currently residing at the jail. We'll make sure it's a private meeting. The other guys don't like seeing an inmate talking to the law. They read all kinds of conspiracy theories into it."

Alastair was impressed with Todd. He was a smart detective who started out as a street cop. He knew his way around an investigation. The rapport between Bill and Todd was evident. Having worked together, they had formed a strong bond. *I never expected this level of support and talent,* thought Alastair, *maybe we can make some progress. Best not tell Marilyn anything until I have something to put on the table. This has been very hard for her and her husband.*

Chapter 16

The Broome County jail is located on Upper Front Street next to SUNY-Broome Community College. The jail is set back off the street. If you're not looking for it, you'd drive right by. The jail is well maintained and has a good reputation in terms of facilities and infrastructure. Not your favorite place to stay but there were a lot worse places around the country. Todd had called ahead to set up the meeting.

Mr. John J. Maloney, a less than happy camper, was nervous as he was taken from his cell to a small room where three men were seated. He had no idea what they wanted and feared the worst. Maybe the cop he hit died or was in the hospital now?

Man, this is not good, he thought, *these guys are going to put me away. Shit, why did I have to take a swing at that cop? He wasn't yelling at me or anything like that. I'm screwed! Three guys and just me? What the hell is going on?*

"I ain't talking with you guys without my lawyer."

Todd said, "Relax, my man, we're not here to talk about your recent arrest."

"So, why are you here and why does it take three guys to talk to a prisoner. I've been here three weeks and ain't had any trouble. I know I screwed up hitting the cop. For what it's worth, I'm real sorry about that. When I get drunk, I get stupid sometimes."

"Maloney, you're a very lucky guy. You assaulted a police officer and knocked him to the ground. He didn't know if you were armed at that point. He could have easily drawn his weapon and who knows what could have happened after that. You're lucky Officer Grant is a cool head and only restrained you. In another place and time, you would have been shot dead," said Bill.

"I know. I really feel bad about this and would like to apologize to the officer."

"That's for later. We're not here about that now," said Todd.

"Look, I'm not a snitch. If you're looking for me to rat out someone here, it ain't going to happen. I keep to myself and don't get involved with the other guys."

Alastair joined the conversation. "John, we're trying to find a young lad who went missing around ten years ago. He probably witnessed the murders of two drug dealers in a lot on the west side. The local guy was part of group selling dope around town. You were in that crew. We're trying to understand how you guys moved drugs in those days. It may help us get a better track on the missing kid."

"Anything you tell us stays in this room. We're not looking to jam you up. We want to understand how the game was played in those days. You were part of it," said Todd.

"Who's the missing kid?"

Todd replied, "His name is Raymond Leonard."

"I remember something about a missing kid back then. Was he involved in the killings?"

"We think he may have seen it go down," said Bill.

"You sure? They would have killed him on the spot," said Maloney, "those dudes were bad news. They didn't take prisoners."

"What happened back then?" asked Bill.

"Look guys, I'll help you, but I sure need some help here with the assault on the cop. I know I'm facing charges but maybe you can talk to the DA and the cop I hit and see if there's any wiggle room."

Todd replied, "We can't make any promises or offer a deal at this point. If you can help us, I'll speak to the DA. I know the cop you assaulted and if the DA is receptive to looking at the charges, I'll speak to him and see how he feels about it. To put any of this into play, we need you to help us out."

"Okay, I understand. Where do you want to start?"

Alastair asked, "How did you guys run your drug business in those days?"

"The market was pretty simple back then. We mainly dealt in marijuana and cocaine. This was before fentanyl and meth. We didn't handle heroin. We were afraid of the dealers, and the junkies who used it were pretty desperate and anything could happen when you were selling to them. The guys who supplied us were really bad news. They wanted us to deal heroin also. We said no way and they beat the crap out of one of our guys. We were five back then. He never really recovered. Went to live with his sister in Albany and died shortly after. I'm sure it was because of the beatings. They used a pipe on his head and kicked him in the chest and stomach. Broken ribs and ruptured spleen. He was a mess. After that, they found some space cadet around Cortland who handled the heroin for them and lost interest in us."

"How big was your territory?" asked Todd.

"We operated around Binghamton and out close to Elmira. We got most of our junk from the city. Sometimes we would get a bigger package and mules would come in and move it on."

"Where'd it go?" asked Alastair.

"Mostly up to Rochester and around there. Sometimes the Rochester mules would go to the city to get their stuff and other times we would meet up with them in Binghamton. I don't know why they did that. Nobody trusted anyone and the game kept changing. We didn't want to be involved in any of the distribution but didn't have a choice. Play their game our they would cut you off and worse."

"Why was your guy killed in the lot that night?" asked Todd.

"The usual reason, territory," replied Maloney, "we did pretty well back then. Never really tried to expand the territory. We were happy with what we had but there was a lot of pushing and shoving back then for territory. In the end, Wayne was killed and we pretty much shut up shop. We couldn't fight a war against those guys. They were connected in the city and were big players in New York state. We had to get out or be killed. No real decision there."

"What happened to the Rochester guys?" asked Todd.

"I don't know. All we did was pass on dope to them when they wanted to use Binghamton as a distribution point. I sort of think the Rochester dealers were connected to the New York City guys, not just buyers. Probably part of their network or family. We were just small-time operators and they wanted us out. They whacked Wayne and that was it."

"What about the other guy with Wayne that night?"

"I'd seen him around a few times. He was a mule from Monticello; they used him to move dope. He wasn't a big player, just another mule."

"Why'd they kill him," asked Todd.

"Who knows, probably because he was there. They were after Wayne, and he was with him. Dead men can't talk."

"Who was the shooter?" asked Bill.

"Someone from the city, I think. Drug killings are usually a mess. Lots of bullets and collateral damage. This was clean. I think they hired someone to do the deed. He wasn't from here, that's for sure, we would know."

Alastair asked, "Tell us what was supposed to go down that night."

"It was supposed to be a simple exchange. The dope was coming up from Monticello and a mule was coming in from Rochester to pick it up. Part of the package was for us but most of it was going to Rochester. We were supposed to meet in the back of that lot over on the west side."

Todd asked, "Did you know the mule from Rochester?"

"I'd worked with him a few times before. Sort of a college kid type of guy. Not your usual mule."

"Got a name?" asked Todd.

"He had one of those last names used for a first name; Reilly, I think. Never heard his last name. I don't think he was with the guys when the shooting went down. He'd be dead if he was there. I don't know if he saw something and ran, or came along after the guys were killed. My guess is that only Wayne and the Monticello guy were in the lot. What makes you think that this Raymond kid was there?"

Alastair replied, "We have some photos from the crime scene and his shopping cart is there. We don't know more than that."

"That's a big jump trying to connect that Raymond kid with the murders. I think you're winging it."

"You may be right," said Todd, "we don't know anything more at this point. We want to talk to people who were there or know how the game was played. Maybe this Reilly guy saw something and can fill in more holes, if we can find him."

After the meeting with John Maloney ended, the three men sat in the conference room discussing the next steps. Maloney had been helpful. They got more information from him than expected.

Todd said, "I'll talk to Officer Grant and the DA about Maloney. Grant's a smart cop. Cutting Maloney some slack may help him later. You're always looking for sources on the street."

"Anyone know any cops up in Rochester?" asked Alastair

Bill replied, "I do and so does Lieutenant Hendricks. We worked a joint operation with them on a loan sharking scam the year before I retired, and I'm pretty sure there's still contact between the departments. The loan sharking case is just coming to trial. I can make some calls, but I think the Lieutenant is a better call. No pun intended guys!"

"Okay," said Todd, "I'll get with the boss and see what he can do. Bill, do you want to stay involved with this? Lots of cards yet to play."

"Sure, my wife is happy to have me out of the house. Maybe I can earn a citizen's crime stoppers badge!"

Chapter 17

Endwell Investigations was growing. Alastair was a good boss. He set up 401K plans for both Chantal and Randy, also a profit-sharing scheme. Finding good people was always a challenge and they fit the model. They were keepers.

Chantal and Randy had made good progress in their research on the blaster and explosives company. When they worked a research project together, they called themselves "the dynamic duo." It always made Chantal laugh. They were a good team. Chantal had a good head for details and kept the data well organized. Randy could be a bit off the wall, but he was creative and that was important when you were stuck in a dead-end place. Alastair had learned to leave them alone to get on with the task. Don't get in the middle, just let them do their work!

Late in the afternoon, they were sitting around the table in the conference room next to the reception area. Sherlock was under the table, resting her head on Alastair's foot. It was a casual review of the current and upcoming cases. They finished their meeting with a review of their two big cases. Finding Raymond Leonard and the quarry accident.

Alastair started the review with Raymond. "We think there's a connection in Rochester that may help us find Raymond or at least get us a bit closer to him. We interviewed a guy the other day at the county jail named John Maloney. He was part of a drug crew in Binghamton back then. He gave us some good background on how the game was played. It looks like a drug mule from Rochester was at or near the lot at the time of the murders. He may have seen something, maybe even Raymond."

"Got a name?" asked Randy.

"Maybe a first name, Reilly," said Alastair, "we're reaching out to the Rochester cops for some help in finding the guy."

"Over nine years is a long time in the drug business," replied Chantal, "he may be long gone. Those guys never really put down roots. Gone or dead would be my guess."

"You're probably right but it's all we have at this point. We'll run it down and see where it takes us. Lieutenant Hendricks is contacting the Rochester cops."

"Most of the police departments have a dedicated group chasing drugs and the cops assigned to them tend to stay together for a long time. You may find there's some good street history from these guys. They may be able to take you back to those days. The cops here have a dedicated drug investigation group. Some of them make it a career. They've helped me out in the past," replied Randy.

"Let's hope. We're waiting on Lieutenant Hendricks to come back to us, and then we can take the next steps."

"Who's the lead?" asked Randy.

"Todd Adams. He used to be Bill Runnings partner. Bill is also helping us. He's retired now but was the lead on the case back in the day."

"Well, there's a great combination," laughed Chantal, "A private investigator, a working detective and a retired detective. The three musketeers ride again. You guys cover all the bases. I like it!"

From there, they turned to the quarry case. Chantal and Randy had been looking into the explosives company and the blaster for over a week.

Randy started, "Being a blaster can be very complicated. All different kinds of terrain and you could be working above and below ground. Our guy pretty much specialized in working blue stone quarries around northern Pennsylvania. He's a local guy named Travis Durgan and only worked this area. I was able to talk to a couple of quarry owners around the area who use him. All of them had good things to say about the guy. He knew how to work bluestone and was very careful."

"Did any of them mention any accidents?"

"No, not at all. In fact, they knew of the Bellmore farm accident and said it made no sense. All of them felt something else was in play. They have confidence in Travis and continue to use him."

"Did Travis ever have any other accidents?"

"I don't think so, it sure didn't come up in the conversations. I'll check back to make sure. The owners said blasting bluestone is pretty straight forward. It's an open area and easily accessible. Apparently, you arrange a series of blasting holes on the bluestone to produce the desired fracture. Sometimes you do a series of blasts to get the results you need. It's not child's play but Travis only works bluestone and knows his trade. Nobody had an issue with him, and this goes back a number of years."

"Okay, thanks. Chantal where are you with the explosives company?"

"They've been around for a long time. Nothing dramatic in their history. They do most of their business in the eastern and southern states. There was a factory accident twenty years ago that took some lives. I couldn't find anything bad about their products. They make a wide range of explosives. It all depends on the type of rock you're blasting and whether its above or below ground. It seems that bluestone is relatively soft so you don't need anything special in terms of explosives. Sort of a standard product from their catalog. Actually, of all the stone, the bluestone is one of the easier ones to work with. Granite is an altogether different game."

"I wonder if there was a storage issue problem with the explosives?" asked Alastair.

Randy replied, "I don't think so. The quarry guys I spoke with told me Travis keeps all his explosives in a secure storage set-up at his farm, a few miles outside of Montrose. Nothing is ever stored at the quarries. He had control of the explosives. I'd bet against any storage issues. I'm just speculating at this point, but I think there was a problem with the product. Something like that. I went over to his place to try and talk with him. He knows that we're working for a law firm retained by the injured guys and he may be sued, so he wouldn't talk about the accident. I don't blame him. I wouldn't talk to me, either! But he did show me how he stores and manages the explosives. I don't think he's some cowboy; he knows the business."

"Well," replied Alastair, "we'll never be able to get close to these guys without a deposition. We have to wait for the lawyers to file and then we can talk to them. Did you talk to any other guys who do blasting around here? Maybe they can provide some more background?"

"Yeah, there's another guy around who does a bit of blasting for the quarries. He's cutting back and I'm told, going to retire soon. He knows Travis. Maybe he'll talk to me. I'll give him a call."

After their meeting, Alastair took Sherlock and the headed over to the driving range at the Enjoie Golf Course. It was about a quarter of a mile from the golf course on the road to the Tri-Cities Airport. Plenty of open space for Sherlock to roam around. When they arrived, she would usually take off in a hurry looking for critters. But after a short time would come back and lie down near Alastair's golf bag and just watch the show. Whenever they went out, Sherlock never went too far away from Alastair. The two had formed a close bond. She slept in his bedroom at the house and was always next to him at the office. Alastair always wondered if the past abuse was still with her. Just memories now or part of her DNA?

While he was there, he ran into Todd Adams. "Hey, crime stopper, getting tuned up for league play day after tomorrow?"

"Sort of. I hate to get on the first tee cold. Anything I can do a day or two ahead makes a difference for me. How about you?"

"Oh, just needed to take a step back from a couple of cases. Sometimes I overthink things and stepping back helps."

"I do that, too. The job can eat you up if you're not careful. My wife, Judy is always reminding me to not forget about my life outside the job. It's a challenge; you lock up one bad boy and two more show up."

"I sure know about that." said Alastair, "When I was with the FBI, we spent months, even years making a case. Sometimes, it was hard to keep it in perspective. You knew who they were and what they were doing but you had to make the case. One of my bosses always compared it to a baseball game. He defined progress in terms of hits, run and errors. Sounds a bit silly but it was really like that. Hard to hit a home run. Lots of singles and our share of strikeouts, too."

"Do you miss the FBI?" asked Todd.

"I used to, but not anymore. The PI business has been very good to me, and I love the variety of assignments. After my wife was murdered, I needed to reinvent myself. I was beat up pretty badly in the ambush in Miami. The bureau would not put me at risk in the field anymore, so the PI business sort of saved me. I'm in a good place now. I'm a happy guy."

Chapter 18

When Alastair and Sherlock got to the office the next day, there was a call waiting from Lieutenant Hendricks. Alastair called back and caught him on the way to a meeting.

"Good morning, Elton, returning your call."

"Hey, Todd told me you were at Enjoie yesterday practicing. Hmm, I need to get serious about my game, you guys are pushing me!"

"Yeah, I ran into Todd. I was there to get away from the office and step back from my two open cases. I'm starting to overanalyze them."

"Oh, boy, always a trap for a cop. Stay with the evidence and let it take you forward. Well, that's what I tell the guys and we all struggle to do it. I got a call back from the Rochester police. Captain Givens is happy to help. There's a couple of guys there who have the history on the drug business back then. Give the captain a call and read him into your investigation. He'll put you with his guys. You may have to go over there and meet with them. I think it's the way to go. No substitute for face-time and you know cops; we love to be smoozed!"

"Should I bring doughnuts?" laughed Alastair.

"Only if they're Krispy Cremes. We cops are fussy eaters!"

Alastair called Captain Givens and briefed him on the case and progress to date. The length of time since Raymond disappeared was a worry to the captain.

"It's such a long time, Mr. Stewart. I hope his mother realizes that the odds are very long on finding him and if we do, the outcome may not be what she is hoping for."

"I've had the conversation with her about this. I think she and her husband understand the situation. I've approached the case in a very segmented manner. We only move forward if we have something to build on. I don't want to take her money and just tickle this. The poor woman is dealing with a recurrence of cancer. She's not sure of her outcome and wants to take another look for her son. I agree with you captain. Even if we can find him, he's probably dead. It's been a long time."

"I've a couple of guys here who go back to those days. Let me review it with them. Can you come over there to meet with us?"

"Absolutely. I'd also like to bring one of my investigators with me if that's Okay."

"Not a problem. Can you also send us a soft copy of your case notes and whatever else you think may be of interest? I want to make sure we're up to speed when we meet."

"Sure, I'll get that out this morning."

"Okay, I'll come back to you with some windows for a meeting."

After the call, Alastair called Raymond's mother. He had made a point of keeping her up to speed on the case. He knew it was always on her mind and wanted to try and alleviate some of her worry.

"Marilyn, we think the two murders in the lot may be tied into the drug trade out of Rochester back then. We interviewed a guy who's in county jail here and was part of a drug crew in Binghamton back then. He told us that there was to be a drug pickup by a person from Rochester the night of the murders. We don't know much more than that now, but it appears that the search field is narrowing. I'm going to go to Rochester shortly and speak with some of the cops who were working drug crimes back then."

"I know you're going to tell me to not get my hopes up, but it does seem positive."

"As I said, the search field appears to be narrowing a bit. We don't know who the guy was who came from Rochester for the drug deal that night or if he saw Raymond at the murder scene. We have to find this guy first and he might be long gone from Rochester. If that's the case, we're at another dead end. I do think it's worth speaking with the Rochester cops and done on a face-to-face basis."

"Should I come with you?"

"You best stay here, I'll keep you posted, promise."

Captain Givens called back the next day.

"How about Thursday or Friday next week?"

"Friday works. My investigator, Randy is in court on Thursday."

"Sure, I'll tell my guys. I'll let the front desk know you're coming."

When Randy came by the office later in the afternoon, Alastair updated him on the Rochester meeting set for the following week.

"I want an extra set of eyes and ears for this meeting. I need you to join me. It's set it up for Friday. We can leave here early Friday morning and be there before ten."

"Let's do it."

"Good. Chantal sent a soft copy of all our notes and case files to Rochester so they should know as much as we do when we meet."

Chapter 19

Before Alastair and Randy left for the meeting in Rochester, he got a call from Baker, Bright & Colson. They had filed a negligence suit against the explosive company, Mid-Atlantic Chemical Company and Trevor Durgan, the blaster. Now they could depose Mid-Atlantic and Trevor, hopefully get closer to the cause of the accident.

"Chantal, would you call Professor McGinn and the University of Scranton and let him know we will be taking his deposition regarding the terrain around the accident site. He may want to have an attorney with him, it's his call. He mentioned that he wanted to take some core samples of the terrain ahead of a deposition. We'll cover the drilling, but we want to know upfront how much it will cost."

"What about the explosives company and the blaster?" asked Randy.

"It's Baker, Bright & Colson's call on the timing," said Alastair, "I'm sure it's right up on the top of their to-do list. They're putting a technical team together for the depositions. Let's see what plays out."

Two days later, Alastair and Randy were on their way to Rochester to meet with the cops who worked the drug scene almost ten years back. The drive to Rochester was an easy trick from Binghamton. They decided to go up I-81N to Syracuse and then over on the NY Thruway to Rochester. Coming back, they would go through the Finger Lakes district. A more scenic ride. Maybe even stop at a winery if they had time. When they arrived at police headquarters, they checked in with the desk sergeant and were taken to a large conference room on the second floor.

"Yikes," said Alastair, "this is a big operation. Must be a lot of bad boys in this town. We better be on our best behavior!"

"Nothing to worry about, Al, we're hard charging detectives from Binghamton. We should have bought our guns so we could show them our fast draw techniques!"

As they were sitting down, Chief Givens came into the room with three of his detectives. Introductions were made and business cards exchanged.

"I'd like to drop by when you finish," said the Chief, "this is very interesting. I hope we can be of some help to you." The Chief then excused himself from the meeting.

Alastair noticed that all the Rochester cops were lieutenants. Clearly, career guys. After some shop talk, Alastair opened up the meeting.

"I see you have our files. Thanks for taking a look at them ahead of the meeting. As you can see, we're trying to find a Raymond Leonard. We think there may have been a connection between Binghamton and Rochester for drug distribution back then, we're hoping that we can narrow the search for Raymond. As you can see, we interviewed a guy from Binghamton who's in our county jail. He was active in a Binghamton drug crew in those days. One of the guys in his crew was murdered in a drug deal gone bad back then. Actually, two people were killed. The Binghamton guy and another from Monticello down in the Catskills. Our guy told us there was a mule from Rochester coming there to pick up some drugs that night. We don't know if the deal fell apart or if it was a robbery. The case was never closed. If we can find the mule from Rochester back then, he may be able to help us. We think the missing lad Raymond was there and saw something."

Lieutenant Gilday, the older of the three men said, "It's odd, they would have killed him on the spot. If he was there and did see something, he must have run away."

"We think so," said Randy, "but we don't know any more than that. If we can find the Rochester mule, we may be able to fill in some open holes."

"Guys don't last a long time in this business. They usually get shot or die from an overdose. It's sort of funny but cops seem to outlast the bad guys. Once we get into this area, we tend to stay. I don't really know why but look at us. Still here and still chasing druggies. We can look at the records back then, maybe something will click. It sure was a busy time even if the market in those days was smaller than now. Back then, there were two established crews moving drugs in Rochester. Also, there was an outlaw biker gang that worked outside of the city. One of the Rochester crews had ties to New York City. We know the drugs came from there or out of Binghamton. I don't think the bikers were in play. They pretty much worked the small towns and villages around here. They got their drugs from Syracuse and Albany."

Alastair asked, "Did the guys who operated in Rochester have a big presence? Mules, dealers and suppliers?"

Lieutenant Gilday responded, "We had good intel on the dealers and suppliers. We knew who they were and could track them. The mules were sort of a shadow group. We only really saw them when we arrested them. They were usually the second-class citizens of the operation. Many of them did it for the drugs. Most of them just happy to be high. Clearly, not a career path for growth within the organization!"

"The guy we interviewed in Binghamton gave us a first name of the Rochester mule who was supposed to have been there that night." said Alastair.

"Let's have it," said one of the lieutenants.

"I only have the first name. Reilly. Not sure of the spelling," said Alastair.

"Give us a minute to check the database. We'll enter it with a couple of spellings," said the lieutenant.

The Rochester cops had a good database and could check information quickly. Not like the old days when you would read case files until your eyes fell out of your head. Now, with a good search engine, the data searches were rapid.

"Bingo!" said Lieutenant Miller who was operating the computer. "We had a guy named Reilly Harrington in for questioning back then. Actually, a couple of times over a two-year period. We were never able to charge him. He seems to have fallen off the radar after that. No other activity that we can see. Most likely he was killed or left the area. Hey, this is interesting! The last time we interviewed the guy, he gave us the name of his girlfriend. Said she could provide an alibi for him. We thought he might be part of a shoot-up between some of the dealers here. I don't know her, but I think she's still around the area. She works for a group of charities. I see her name in the paper every once in a while doing fund raising. Her name is Maria Marchetti."

"Can we speak to her?" asked Alastair.

"Let me find her number and see what we can do," said the Lieutenant Gilday, "it's been over ten years now. We may be opening old wounds."

The lieutenant called Maria and a meeting was set for the early afternoon. Maria was very worried about the upcoming meeting and needed to be careful about providing information to Alastair. When they called her to set up the meeting, they were vague about the reason for the meeting other than they were trying to find a missing boy. When he mentioned the missing boy, she knew it was Raymond. What else could it be? Maybe someone in one of the halfway houses? Not likely, she didn't deal with individual clients. She knew in her heart that it was about Raymond. She was afraid what a change might do to him.

Could he handle it after all these years? He never looked back on his life after coming to Rochester with Reilly. Opening up this part of his life and the traumatic events in Binghamton so long ago may be more than he could handle. He could end up in a dark place with no way out.

She called Reilly who was just finishing up a home care visit to let him know about the meeting.

"Reilly, there's a private investigator from Binghamton here looking for a missing boy! I'm sure it's Raymond. He met with the cops here and has your name."

"Oh, God, what am I going to do? How did he find me?"

"The cops said they found you through some old police records from when you were involved with the drug guys. I think I provided an alibi for you or something like that. My name was in their records and they contacted me. They want to meet with me this afternoon."

"Am I in trouble? Are they going to arrest me for kidnapping? What will they do to Raymond? I don't think he can handle any of this!"

"Reilly, you've done nothing wrong. Raymond was a young man when he came to Rochester with you. If anything, you've saved his life and more. Look how well he's doing. You didn't kidnap a child. You saved a man's life. I'm going to meet with this investigator today and hear what he has to say."

"Oh, great, and the first question will be do you know where I am. What are you going to say?"

"I don't know at this point. I'll tell him something. Right now, we need to understand his game. Why is he looking for Raymond after ten plus years? Why now? Let me hear what he has to say. We'll talk later today."

"Please don't give anything up until we know more."

"Trust me, Reilly, we're on the same page with this."

Alastair and Randy met with Maria at her office, not far from the police station. They decided that the Rochester Police would not be part of the meeting. There was no evidence of a crime having been committed. So, no reason for their presence. Also, they felt the meeting would be more productive If they were not involved at this point.

Although Maria was cordial to Alastair and Randy, the two men could sense a guardedness in her demeanor. She didn't know what the men wanted but it seemed they had connected a lot of the dots. As the meeting started, a call came in for Maria which she had to take. Alastair and Randy excused themselves from the office to let her have some privacy.

While they were waiting for the call to end, Randy leaned over and said, "Al, she's not comfortable with us. We're getting close to something; I can feel it."

"Yeah, let's go slow and not push her. We need her on our side."

When they returned to Maria's office, she explained, "Sorry about that; it was a foundation calling to let us know they had approved our grant request. We're always looking for money. Story of my working life."

"Maria, let me give you some background on why we're here. I was retained by Marilyn Leonard who lives in Binghamton to try and find her son Raymond who went missing almost ten years ago. She's a cancer survivor but it's apparently returned. Although her prognosis is very good, she is worried and wants to try one more time to find her son. We think he may have witnessed a double homicide in Binghamton back then. We don't know that for a fact but we did find solid evidence that he was at the crime scene. It was a drug deal gone bad or maybe a robbery. We don't know. However, we are pretty sure that the meeting that night involved a person who was there from Rochester to pick up drugs from the Binghamton crew. We interviewed a Binghamton person who was part of the drug crew back then and he remembers that night and the meeting. He gave us a first name, Reilly, but didn't know the last name."

Randy noticed that Maria stiffened ever so slightly. Did her breathing become a little more rapid also?

Oh, yeah, you know him, thought Randy.

"As you know in our meeting with the Rochester Police this morning, we reviewed their files regarding drug cases. As I said we only had a first name, Reilly. The cops ran the name and we came across a Reilly Harrington. The Rochester cops had him in for questioning a few times. During one of the interrogations, he gave your name to support his alibi. We want to find Mr. Harrington and see if he can help us find Raymond. Can you help us?"

Maria was clearly disturbed. After all these years it was all on the table.

She thought, *I can't deny a mother access to her child but if Raymond is not able to go back to those days and understand them, it will destroy him. So many years have gone by, we need to be careful in how we open this up. I can't just say, Raymond, your mother called and wants to see you. What am I to do? I need some help!* Maria was quiet for quite a long time. So much that Randy thought something was wrong with her. She was trying to understand what was happening and more importantly, what she should do. She was not about to turn this over to social services and hope for the best. Reilly and Raymond would be cannon fodder in the system. Reilly could even face criminal charges and for what? Saving a person's life? *No, that's not going to happen,* she thought, *I need to sort out a way forward before we take the next steps.*

Finally she spoke to the men. "I need to talk with a therapist I work with here at the foundation. I have the answers you're looking for but need to talk about the impact of this information. People's lives could be ruined or worse if we don't handle this correctly. I can tell you categorically that Raymond is thriving and is in a good place. He's not at risk. You're going to have to trust me, Mr. Stewart."

"Maria, all of us are in uncharted waters now. I'll trust you and ask you to trust me and Randy. This is not a police investigation. However,

I need to verify that Raymond is safe and not at any risk. If you'll help me do this, then we'll pull back and give you time to meet with the therapist and talk with Reilly. But I need to tell Marilyn that we've found her son and he's safe. She's been grieving for years."

"Mr. Stewart, I'm going to give you the name of a home care service called Evercare. Reilly owns the business. They have an office over in Victor. It's a small town near here. I'm going to go there now and will be there when you arrive. I want you to speak to the man at the desk and ask about home care for your aged mother. Reilly is out on a case and won't be back until later tonight. I'm picking up Raymond and taking him home. It's three o'clock now, so plenty of time. The office is only twenty minutes away."

"Okay, I think that's a good plan. I'll be there a little in front of four. What time do they close?"

"Usually around five."

When the two men arrived at the strip mall, they easily located the Evercare office. The office was at the end of a small strip mall. There were six other businesses located there. Four were retail along with a large dental practice at one end of the mall and Evercare at the other end. They sat in the car talking about the next steps before Alastair went in.

"Randy, you hang out here. Take a few pictures of the mall and office. I may show them to Marilyn. What do you think? Is she gaming us?"

"No, I don't think so. If she was, she would have given us a phony address or just stonewalled us. I think she's trying to make this work."

When Alastair went into the Evercare Office, he was met by a smiling man sitting behind a desk who was entering data into his computer. Maria was there talking to Raymond. She excused herself and went into the office in the back.

"I'll wait in Reilly's office, Raymond, so you can talk. Call me if you need me."

Alastair asked Raymond about the care services they offered. Raymond produced a well-designed brochure describing the Evercare services.

"This is a very nice brochure. You found a good company to produce it."

"Reilly and I did most of the initial design." said Raymond. "Premier Graphics in Rochester printed it. We really like it. We update it at least twice a year."

"How long have you been in business?" asked Alastair.

"We started out in our house and then as the business grew, moved here. I guess close to ten years now."

"Do you like it here?"

"Oh, yes, this is my home. Reilly and Maria are my friends. We do lots of things together!"

Raymond and Alastair spent the next thirty minutes reviewing the brochure and talking about the Rochester area. During that time, Alastair was able to get a good feeling about Raymond and his environment. *He's in a good place. Not at risk,* he thought. He thanked Raymond for his time and got up to leave. As he was leaving, Maria came out of the office. He said goodbye to them and left. Alastair went to his car and called Maria on her mobile.

"I understand this a lot better now. He's in a good place and we need to move carefully to bring them all together."

"I'll speak with Doctor Generelli at the Foundation tomorrow and come back to you. I hope Raymond's mother can accept that her son is well and that the next steps are very important."

"I'll speak with her as soon as I get back. I want Randy to take a picture of Raymond as you leave the office. We are off to the side and Randy has a digital camera with a telephoto lens. You won't see us. The photo will help when I see his mother."

As Raymond and Maria left the office, she looked around the parking lot and spotted Alastair's car. There were very few cars in the lot at this time and he was parked off to the side. She made a point of stopping to talk to Raymond about something and made sure he was facing Alastair's car.

"Damn, Randy, I'm so tempted to follow them and see where Raymond lives but I don't want to risk breaking the trust with Maria. She's the glue in this puzzle now."

"Damn straight, don't screw the pooch!"

It was too late in the day for a leisurely drive through the Finger Lakes so they hopped back on the Thruway to Syracuse and on to I-81 south to Binghamton. There was not a lot of conversation between the men on the way back. Each reviewing the day's events and pondering the next steps. *Maybe finding Raymond was the easy part, now the hard work begins?* thought Alastair, *I hadn't really considered how this would impact Raymond. I sort of thought we would connect him with his parents and declare victory. This is a new ballgame. We never thought much about Raymond other than finding him. What if he doesn't want to see his parents? Then what do we do? Man, I don't see a straight line forward yet.*

Alastair went over to see Marilyn with the news as soon as they got back. "We found Raymond and he's doing well. Safe and happy. He lives with a man who rescued him when he first came to Rochester. He's looked after him all these years. I have a picture of Raymond; we took it today. The man who took him in, Reilly Harrington, runs a home care business and Raymond is the office manager and administrative guy."

"Oh, my God! Al, you did it! You found him! When can I see my boy?"

"Soon, I promise, but first we need to meet with the people who are part of Raymond's life now and also a therapist from Rochester to chart out the next steps. I know this is asking a lot, Marilyn, but it's very important that we move carefully and take a step at a time.

Chapter 20

After Alastair and Randy left Rochester to go back to Binghamton, Maria called Reilly. As Maria debriefed him on the meeting with Alastair, Reilly was in a panic.

"Oh, this is awful! They'll take Raymond away from us. It will kill him. We can't let this happen. Why did you let him see Raymond? He'll call the police and they'll take Raymond away and put us all in jail!"

"Reilly, slow down. The private detective understands the situation. Nobody is doing anything like that. We all know how delicate the situation is with Raymond, and we all want to protect him. I'm going to set up a meeting with Doctor Generelli. He's the therapist I've worked with at the foundation for a number of years. We need to chart a way forward for Raymond. I want you with me at the meeting."

"Okay. I guess I've always known this day was coming. I'm really worried for Raymond. He only lives in the present. I've never been able to get him to think or talk of the past. Gave up trying a long time ago. He's a happy guy in his world and we need to protect him."

"We will, I promise," replied Maria.

When Reilly and Maria met with the doctor, the doctor was surprised at the circumstances surrounding Raymond coming to Rochester with Reilly. Initially, it didn't seem to make much sense. You would have expected Raymond to be placed with social services.

However, Doctor Generelli had worked in the system for a number of years and understood the problems they faced.

"I believe we're dealing with two major issues here," the doctor said, "a mother who longs to find her son and a traumatic experience that Raymond is not equipped to handle yet. Trying to deal with them at the same time would be very risky and I doubt that it's even possible. The first thing we should try to do is introduce Raymond to his family. Let's start with his mother and introduce his father later. I don't want to overwhelm him. It's important that he not be taken out of his living and working environment with Reilly. It's an established relationship and role. We don't want to disturb it. I hope his family understands this and does not think they can come in and just take him back to Binghamton. His life is here now."

Maria replied, "I think the detective, Alastair Stewart, from Binghamton, has a good relationship with Raymond's mother and can have the right conversation with her."

"Okay, then the next step is for all the parties to meet and agree on an approach. Raymond's mother and father as well as the three of us. Also, the detective should be part of the meeting. I think it's best if we meet in Binghamton. Meeting in Rochester may be too hard for the parents. Their son would be so close."

Maria called Alastair and a meeting was set up The following week on a warm sunny day, Reilly, Maria, and Doctor Generelli drove to Binghamton and met with Marilyn and Hubert at Endwell Investigations. Reilly had an excellent relationship with his next-door neighbors who gladly agreed to look after Raymond for the day. The biggest challenge would be to get Raymond's parents to understand that their son was in a very good place. Removing him from Reilly would be a major step backwards. Doctor Generelli spent a good deal of time explaining the situation and how they had to move forward in incremental steps.

"Mrs. Leonard, Raymond enjoys a good productive life. Reilly and Maria have taken excellent care of him. He's made a lot of progress. This is his life now. You can certainly be a part of it, but it will take some time. You have to look at him now as a grown man who has moved out of your house and is on his own, so to speak. When we introduce you back into his life, there is a risk that it may trigger the traumatic events of the past. I'll stay close by Raymond during these initial phases. Our objective is to bring his parents back into his life. First the mother and then his father. If we can do that, then maybe over time he can address the murders in Binghamton."

Marilyn Leonard replied, "So I'll visit him and see where it goes?

"Yes, pretty much. He'll accept you and go as far back as he is capable of at this time. As the relationship develops, you can address more issues. For now, imagine you're visiting your grown son who lives in Rochester. I don't think I'm oversimplifying the situation. Your son will set the pace."

Reilly asked, "How do we tell him that his mother wants to see him? As Maria said earlier, do we just say, your mother called and wants to visit?"

"Not that simple," replied the doctor. "I'll meet with Raymond ahead of any of this to assess how stable he is and if he can understand his mother is coming back into his life. If he can't deal with it now, then I'll need to work with him and see if we can get him to a point where he can. I'm hoping we can keep the parents separate from the trauma of the murders. If we can do that, then we have a pretty good way forward."

Alastair joined the conversation. "Marilyn, Hubert, this is going to be a long road. So much has happened. You need to be patient. I know this is asking a lot after all these years, but I think the doctor is right."

"Just knowing that Raymond is safe and thriving after all these years is a dream come true. Marilyn and I know we have a long road ahead," said Hubert. He looked over to Reilly and Maria and said, "Thank you for saving Raymond."

Doctor Generelli said, "Reilly, I'll come over to your office next week to meet Raymond. I want to see him in his work environment. If things look good, we can ask him if his mother can come to Rochester and visit with him."

"Sounds pretty easy," said Maria, "but we're walking through a minefield now."

"Indeed," said the doctor, "that's a good way to look at it."

Chapter 21

While Alastair and Riley were in Rochester, the wheels were turning on the lawsuit recently filed against Trevor Durgan and the explosives company. Baker, Bright & Colson wanted to depose the blaster and manufacturer quickly. Depositions were important to understand the circumstances of the accident and also to establish liability. It was part of the discovery process.

A few days after filing the lawsuit, letters were sent out scheduling the depositions. The lawyers decided to depose Trevor Durgan first. They knew that the explosives company, Mid-Atlantic Chemical Company would have an army of lawyers at their deposition and the odds of speaking with anyone with on-the-ground knowledge of the accident was slim. Mid-Atlantic would be using a scorched-earth strategy. All assistance short of actual help. They felt Trevor would be more likely to provide real information. Based on what Alastair had uncovered from Professor McGinn, the feeling was that Trevor was competent and probably not the source of the problem.

Trevor's deposition took place at the offices of Baker, Bright & Colson in downtown Binghamton. It was a real surprise when Trevor showed up with a heavy-hitter criminal attorney from Philadelphia. Alastair was part of the team taking the deposition along with the lead attorney and Professor McGinn. *Wow! Is there something here we don't understand,* thought Alastair, *Trevor's guy doesn't do house closings and wills, he plays in the big leagues. What's going on here. Did we miss something with Trevor?*

As the attorneys were doing the usual rack-and-stack of each other, trying to assess their importance, Trevor spoke up. "Floyd Gibson, my attorney, is an old Army buddy. He went on to law school after the Army. We were both demolition specialists. He was the smart guy in our platoon!"

"Don't I wish!" laughed Floyd, "I'm based in Philadelphia and do mostly criminal law. When Trevor called, I was happy to support him. We'll try to answer your questions."

After the formalities of identifying the people in the room and discussing the ground rules, they started the deposition. A stenographer was there to take down their testimony. Henry McArdle, the lead attorney for Baker, Bright & Colson opened the questions. He spent a lot of time reviewing Trevor's background and experience in the quarry blasting business. *Interesting,* thought Floyd, *they're spending a lot of time confirming that Trevor is established and competent. They must be looking somewhere else for the cause.* After about twenty minutes of questioning, Floyd asked for a quick break to speak with Trevor. He wanted to make sure he understood the evolving strategy.

"Trev, my sense is that they're not after you. I don't know what other information they have but I think they suspect that the liability doesn't rest with you. We want to cooperate with these guys but we don't have to stand here with our pants at our ankles and ask them to be gentle! I'll give you guidance on how to deal with their questions if it's needed. They brought us in first and that's telling."

"Do you think they're after the explosives company?" asked Trevor.

"Who's left? Must be them. They didn't file against the farm owner, Ted Bellmore."

When they resumed the deposition, Henry McArdle turned the questioning over to Professor McGinn, and Alastair who asked about the more technical aspects of the blasting process.

"Trevor, tell us how you set up a blasting site," asked the professor, "for example, assessing the terrain and deciding on where to drill the holes for the explosives."

"Even if I know the site from past work, I always do a walk through. I approach it as if I'm working the quarry for the first time. The guys are working the quarry face all the time and even if there isn't any more blasting, things change as they take out the stone. You have to look at it as a new site every time."

"I assume you worked on that site before?" asked Alastair.

"Many times, it was a good one. I've been blasting there for a number of years."

"How many?" asked his attorney.

"At least eight years."

"Did you ever have an issue there?" asked the professor.

"No, never. As these quarries go, this was a very stable one. We could work on the top and bottom of it. The whole face was solid bluestone."

"Tell us about the bore holes for blasting," asked the professor.

"It all depends on what you want to move," said Trevor, "you place the holes to get the desired results. Sometimes, you have to blast an area a second time to get what you want. Once it's done, I inspect the area to make sure it's safe and then the crews can come in and get the stone. Before we set the initial blasts, we clear the area. I'm usually off to the side and one of the quarrymen is in a safe area with the guys. We never set off a blast until we're sure all the guys have been accounted for."

"Is this a risk issue?" asked Alastair.

"The area near the blast is always cleared of personnel. Usually, the guys are in the shop. No real reason for them to be around the blasting site. But you never know. That's why I always have a quarryman helping to make sure we don't have any strays, as we call them."

"What happened on the day of the blast?" asked the professor.

"Mr. Bellmore had some new guys. Recent hires. He wanted them to see the blasting process. Not that they would be part of it, but just to show them that end of the business. Sort of an orientation. They were back with my safety man in the safe zone. When I set off the explosives, it was much bigger than we usually get or certainly planned to get. A major part of the quarry face blew out and scattered a lot of debris. As you know, some of it hit the guys."

Alastair said, "Can you tell us what you think happened?"

"When you blast bluestone, you don't get a lot of flying debris, if any. Mostly, it's a loud thumping sound and a vibration you can feel in the ground. It's not very dramatic. Sort of a pulsing felt from the ground and maybe a bit of a shift on the face, opening up new fractures. I usually drill five to seven bore holes. When we set off this one, it was different. A large vibration felt through the ground and also an upward ejection of a lot of debris."

"Why?" asked Alastair.

"It was like I was using a more powerful explosive. Much more powerful. I checked my invoice from Mid-Atlantic and also the markings on the sticks. It's the same stuff I've been buying for years from them. It's color coded and has a good tracking process. Batch number, production number, etc."

"Did you use all of the sticks?"

"No, it was a new purchase. I got it a week before I used it. I kept it in my storage locker at my farm. I must have two-thirds of it left. "

At that point, Trevor's attorney, Floyd Gibson spoke up.

"I think we are both headed in the same direction. We'll test the remaining explosives. We can make some of it available to you if you also want to do testing. I recommend that we test independently. If there's an issue with the explosives, Mid-Atlantic should also test and we need to be on solid footing. It appears at this point that there may be an issue with the explosives, but I don't want to get ahead of myself."

Henry McArdle, the lead attorney from Baker, Bright & Colson responded.

"I agree, Floyd. We would like to go with you to Trevor's farm to get a sample for testing. I want to establish a good chain of custody and control

I'm concerned about storage. Can Trevor isolate them in a separate location?"

"My storage is secure and meets all the state requirements. I don't have much in my storage locker now. I only buy what I plan to use in the near future. I could move the other explosives to a colleague who does blasting around here if you want to keep them apart. My locker is secure and is the best place for the explosives."

Chapter 22

Alastair went to Trevor's farm along with Floyd Gibson to get samples of the explosives for testing. He was concerned about handling the material and sending it to the testing lab located outside of Boston.

"It's safe, Mr. Stewart," said Trevor, "there aren't any fuses attached. Just keep it dry and in a reasonable temperature environment. Use a courier service to get it to the lab. I'd like both of you to test four sticks. I have over a dozen in the locker. I'll keep the remaining sticks just in case we need to provide them to the blasting company."

"Why four?" asked Floyd.

"I don't know. Just a feeling that there may be some discrepancies in the manufacturing process, and I want to make sure we take a good look at it," said Trevor.

"Are those the colored rings around the sticks that you spoke about earlier when we were at the office?" asked Alastair.

"Yes, it's another way of identifying the explosives. They have all that information printed on them but the color coding is a backup way to identifying them in case the on-site conditions are not good. Maybe poor light, weather, stuff like that."

"Does the color coding and writing on them match?" asked Alastair.

"Yeah, it sure does. I've been using this stuff for years. Nothing's changed. I also checked it against the invoice to make sure it all matches."

"So, no surprises?" asked Alastair.

"No, it all tracked."

"What do we tell the labs to do?" asked Floyd.

"Two things for sure," said Trevor, "you want an analysis of their strength. That means a controlled explosion of the material. Also, a chemical analysis of the explosives. We need to understand if something went wrong when it was manufactured."

Both Floyd and Alastair left the farm with four sticks of explosives each. Floyd had made arrangements to drop his sample with a lab near Philadelphia on his way back to the office. Alastair would be sending his explosives by courier the next day. It would probably be a few weeks before they had the results.

When he got back to the office, Chantal and Sherlock were waiting for him. Chantal had the same reaction to the explosives as Alastair did when he first saw them. Are they safe? Will they explode? How do we handle them?

"Can you just leave them in the office overnight?" asked Chantal.

"Yeah, I'm going to lock them in my desk. The courier will be here at eight-thirty tomorrow and take them over to the lab near Boston. They asked the same questions you just did. They're safe. But it's sort of scary having the dynamite here. Hell, I don't even keep my gun in the office."

Sherlock was quite interested in the explosives and kept sniffing them.

"Al," laughed Chantal, "I bet she thinks they're something to eat!"

"Be careful, Sherlock," said Alastair, "you can get a really bad case of indigestion!"

Chapter 23

Doctor Generelli was pleasantly surprised when he met Raymond at Evercare in Victor, just outside of Rochester. The Evercare business had a reception area where Raymond worked. It was neat and well organized. All Raymond's doing, said Reilly. There was a well-appointed conference room and Reilly's office was behind the reception area.

When the doctor arrived, the office had just closed for the day. Raymond was at his workstation in the reception area closing down the computer and finishing up some open files. Reilly was in his office in the back.

"I'm sorry but we're just closing, can I help you?" said Raymond.

"That's okay, Reilly is expecting me; can you tell him I'm here?"

As they were talking Reilly came out of his office. He was dressed in scrubs. He usually spent two days a week with the teams as they made their calls.

"Hi, Doc, just got back a few minutes ago. Have you been waiting long?"

"Not at all, I just arrived. I believe this is Raymond; he's been very helpful."

"More than helpful to our business, he runs the admin side. If you need help with a spreadsheet, I've got the man for you."

"I may take you up on that; my scheduling's a mess."

Raymond could sense that something was happening but was not sure what it could be. He asked the doctor why he was here.

"Is Reilly sick? He didn't say anything to me."

"No, Reilly is fine. I'm not a physician. I'm a doctor who helps people deal with, and understand, difficult things in their lives. I'm called a therapist. Reilly wants to ask you a question and I'm here to help the both of you if it's necessary."

Raymond was confused. He didn't understand what was going on.

Reilly explained to Raymond that Doctor Generelli was the kind of doctor who helped people understand themselves and deal with difficult issues in their life. Maybe Raymond did not fully comprehend the explanation, but he was comfortable with the doctor.

Reilly said, "Don't worry, Raymond. Everything is fine and nothing will change. We're a team and will always be together. Maria and I will always be here with you."

Reilly held his breath for a few seconds and then started. "I need to ask you a question. Is that okay?"

"Sure, but is something wrong? Are we in trouble?"

"No, not at all. You might remember a time before you lived with Reilly, when you were young? You lived in Binghamton? Your mom and dad lived with you? Well, your mother would like to come to Rochester and visit with you. Is that okay?"

Doctor Generelli could see that Raymond was trying to process a lot of memories from his time back then. The good news was that he didn't panic or get emotional. He was trying to understand what had just happened. Reilly was looking intently at Raymond, hoping for a sign of understanding or acceptance.

"I don't want to go back there. The bad man will hurt me. I want to stay here with Reilly, in our house!" exclaimed Raymond.

"You can always stay with Reilly. This is your home. We will never take it away from you," said Doctor Generelli, "you're safe here with Reilly and Maria."

"My mother and father will be mad at me for running away," exclaimed Raymond, "I know I made them sad but the bad men were trying to hurt me."

Reilly spoke, "Raymond, your mother will be overjoyed to see you again after all this time. Your mother and father never forgot you and never stopped looking for you. They love you and want to see you again."

"Raymond, would it be okay if your mother came to visit you and Reilly next week? Maybe on Saturday?" asked Doctor Generelli.

"Will you be here also?" asked Raymond, "I'm scared."

"Yes" said the doctor, "and Reilly will be here, too!"

After the meeting, Doctor Generelli called Alastair. "Al, it looks like we made some good progress today. Can you bring Marilyn over here on Saturday, next week? Reilly and I spoke with Raymond and he wants to meet his mother. I still think it's best to start with Marilyn first and then introduce his father on the next visit. I'm worried about the emotional impact of all of this. I think we're in a good place, but we must be careful going forward or we'll lose the progress we've made. Let's plan on one o'clock in the afternoon and see how it goes. Please caution Marilyn to let Raymond take the lead. I don't know how open he'll be or what level of conversation they can have. We just have to let this play out. Please make sure Marilyn understands that this is the first of many steps. Get here a bit ahead of one, so I can talk with you and Marilyn before we go into their house."

"I'll call her now and give her the news on the visit. I'll take the opportunity to talk about how you want to move forward. I hope her husband doesn't have a problem with being left at home for the first visit. You know what, Doc? I think I'll go over to the house and talk about this in person. This is a big step for them and best handled on a face-to-face basis."

"Thanks, Al," I appreciate your concern.

Alastair called ahead and Marilyn and Hubert were waiting for him when he pulled into the driveway. Their house on the west side of Binghamton was in a well-established neighborhood. Although an older house, it had been modernized and updated over the years. Vinyl siding, new roof, windows, and the garage now connected to the house by a breeze-way. The lawn and garden were well maintained. *Must be a lawn care service,* thought Alastair, *it would be pretty much a full-time job to do it yourself.*

Before he could ring the bell, Marilyn opened the door, a big smile on her face.

"Al, is this really happening? I won't sleep a wink before next Saturday. I'm glad you're driving, I'm too nervous to drive. I don't think Hubert and I have felt such joy for years."

"You always need a bit of luck in this business and we had some. I'm so happy for the two of you. I trust Hubert is on-board with not coming for the first visit?"

Hubert joined Marilyn. "It's fine with me, Al. I think we need to follow Doctor Generelli's direction. I'd love to be there, but as you said earlier, one step at a time."

Marilyn asked, "Should I bring anything from Raymond's room? Clothes, books, pictures?"

"No, just yourself. Raymond will take the lead on how involved he wants to be in these early stages. He'll prompt you on what to do. Trust him. One point that Doctor Generelli recommends is you emphasize that nothing will change in Raymond's life. That his job, relationship with Reilly and Maria, and most important, where he lives won't change. He's still traumatized by the murders and does not want to go back to Binghamton. He has a very productive life in Rochester. He's in a good, safe place. The strategy is to be a part of his life, not replace it."

"We understand, Al. The fact that he's safe and happy is all that matters."

Chapter 24

Early the following week, Baker, Bright & Colson deposed Mid-Atlantic, the explosives manufacturer. As before, Henry McArdle had briefed Alastair and the Professor about the strategy for the deposition. He would handle the general questions and they would handle the detailed questions. He warned the Professor to expect Mid-Atlantic to question his credentials. He told the Professor to not push back on this, just deflect the accusations. It was a smoke screen.

Mid-Atlantic came in with a full legal team and all guns blazing. They'd done nothing wrong, end of story. The company representatives and their lawyers sat there not offering any constructive comments and refusing to talk in any detail about the accident. As best they could, they tried to limit their answers to a simple yes or no. Alastair had the feeling that Mid-Atlantic was also looking in the same place they were for the cause of the accident. That is the manufacturing process. When Baker, Bright & Colson asked them if they had changed or planned to change any of their manufacturing or quality control processes, Alastair could sense a change in the demeanor of some of the Mid-Atlantic people. If they found anything, they were not about to give it up.

The results from the independent lab testing had not arrived yet but Alastair and Professor McGinn were comfortable that there was an issue with the manufacturing or coding of the explosives. The team asked for copies of their manufacturing and quality control standards. Mid-Atlantic grudgingly agreed to provide them. When Alastair also asked for a copy of their earlier ones, he could feel the tension among the Mid-Atlantic people. If they had made any recent changes, it would show up.

Unsurprisingly, the deposition ended on a sour note. Alastair and Professor McGinn asked Mid-Atlantic if they did any explosive testing as part of their quality control or as a result of the accident. Their vice president for manufacturing went into a long dissertation on their processes and how thorough there were. After some minutes of listening to the gentleman, Alastair interrupted him and said, "Just answer the question the same way you've been doing all morning. Yes or No. How hard is that?"

The vice president of manufacturing again attempted to explain their great processes. Alastair cut him off.

"I'll take that as a no!" replied Alastair sharply.

After the deposition, Alastair and Professor McGinn went over to Starbucks which was nearby. The professor did not have any classes scheduled for the day, so he wasn't in any rush to head back to Scranton. Both men felt that something went wrong when they made the explosives or they were simply mislabeled. Either way, it would explain the accident. But they needed evidence and Mid-Atlantic was clearly in a defensive posture. They'd circled the wagons.

"Well, Al, until we hear from the labs, all we can do is drink coffee and speculate. We should have something next week. If Mid-Atlantic haven't tested the explosives in the production run ahead and behind Trevor's buy, they're damn fools. Test what you have in inventory and notify your other customers who bought it. Someone else could get hurt. I don't trust their VP of Manufacturing. He's in denial. This accident could take these guys to their knees! Not just company liability, but personal liability, too!"

Alastair replied, "It sort of reminds me of Nixon and Watergate. Deny, deny, deny and hope it goes away. In the end, it'll take you down. Does every time."

"What does the rest of your week look like at Endwell Investigations?"

"I'm off to Rochester for a meeting on Saturday. We're also taking on a case involving insurance fraud. It's a busy time at the office. I'm going to get scarce on Friday afternoon and hit the golf course. Other than that, dinner with my sister and her boys on Friday. Both in college now at Union in Schenectady. Home for the weekend to do two months of laundry and enjoy mom's cooking. They're a hoot! I love being around them."

"Find some time and come down to Scranton, we can play some golf. We have some very good courses around there. I play with a great group of retired teachers and school administrators. You'd really enjoy their company. By the way, I'm very good!"

"You are?"

"No, but I live in hope!"

"Yikes, that sounds familiar. Let's see what we can put together. I'd love to play with your group. Let's set something up."

Well, thought Alastair, *big weekend coming up. I hope Raymond can process everything that's happening. Doctor Generelli has been a great resource. Quite a calming influence on us all. Marilyn is so nervous about the meeting. If it doesn't go well, she'll be crushed. But her son is safe and that is the main point, I guess. I don't have much play in the meeting other than to drive the car and support Marilyn. So maybe I'll take Sherlock along. She loves rides in the car. It might take Marilyn's mind off the visit for a bit.*

On a cloudy Saturday morning, around nine-thirty, Alastair and Marilyn were on the way to Rochester. First a quick stop at a Starbucks on Front Street for some coffee and a bagel then onto I-81N up to Syracuse and west on the NY Thruway. Traffic was light. Alastair put his car on cruise control and followed the moving line of traffic.

Marilyn did not say much on the way up I-81 to Syracuse. She was lost in her thoughts imaging various outcomes. Alastair could sense her fear but felt he best not talk about it and let her process the issues. As they came into Syracuse and were passing the Carrier Dome used by the university for sports events, she said "Al, I 'm so worried that Raymond will not want to talk to me. What can I do is he shuts me down?

"Talk to Doctor Generelli."

"He may be angry and tell me to go away, what can I do?"

"Talk to Doctor Generelli."

"Okay, I get your point. Sorry to be such a worrywart."

"That's to be expected, Marilyn. We're in uncharted waters now. My sense is that because Raymond agreed to meet with you, he wants to reconnect in some manner. If he didn't, I don't think he would have agreed to a meeting. Just be yourself and see what happens. Trust Doctor Generelli."

The rest of trip was uneventful. Alastair filled Marilyn in on Reilly Harrington and his home care business and relationship with Raymond. Most of it she knew from the earlier meeting in Binghamton, but Alastair wanted to keep the conversation going and hopefully alleviate some of her anxiety.

"You know, they've been together since the murders. Somehow they met up at the bus station and Reilly looked after him. He took him in. They've been together all these years. Reilly's long-time girlfriend, Maria, is also a big part of Raymond's life. It's pretty much the three of them. Sorry, I guess most of this you already know."

"That okay, Al, it's comforting to hear. What exactly does Raymond do in the business?"

"From what Reilly told us, he's the office manager, scheduler, and the first voice the clients hear when they contact the agency. I know that they use a CPA to manage the books, but Raymond is the bookkeeper for the day-to-day running of the firm. This isn't a make-work type of job, he's important to the operation. Reilly really depends on him."

"I can see why he doesn't want to leave. I don't want to try and take him back to Binghamton. He's safe and happy in Rochester. I just want to be part of his life. I hope he'll let me in."

Chapter 25

Reilly and Raymond lived about five miles away from their office, also in Victor. Their house was on a cul-de-sac bordering open land at the back of the house. A bit like Alastair's house in Endwell with open land at the back. The neighborhood was well established. The houses were built as part of a development around 2000. It was a three-bedroom house with a finished basement and a deck on the back. It had a two-car garage attached to the house. New vinyl siding and windows had been installed about five years ago. Reilly had good neighbors on both sides who had pretty much adopted Raymond.

Alastair and Marilyn arrived about thirty minutes early. Alastair had built in a bit of a buffer in their travel time to Victor as he didn't want to be late.

"Let's drive over to their office. It's not far from here. We have some time to spare. I can show you the operation at least from outside the front door."

Evercare fit well into the small strip mall. A front window and door faced the parking lot. A simple sign above the window identified the business. On the door was a sign with hours of operation and emergency phone numbers. A professional presentation.

"Looks nice," Marilyn said, "you get a good feeling looking at it."

"I think they've been here about eight years. In the early days, they ran the business from their house. As the business grew, they moved here. Let's get back to the house, Doctor Generelli should be there by now. He wants to meet with us before we go in."

When they turned into the cul-de-sac, the doctor was parked off to the side. He waved them over to his car.

"I wanted to see how you're doing before we meet Raymond. We'll all go in together and I'll introduce you to him. Reilly you already met from our earlier meeting. Maria won't be there. We want to keep the numbers down for the initial visit. As best you can, Al, you and Reilly should excuse yourself from the meeting. Then it will be Raymond, his mother and me."

"Sure, I've got my dog with me, Reilly and I can take her for a walk."

Reilly answered the door when they rang the bell. "Doctor, Alastair, Mrs. Leonard, nice to see you again. Looking at Marilyn he said, "welcome to our house."

When they entered the house, they were in a small narrow hall. There was a side table there where the mail, keys, and notes were kept so the group had to go into the living room single file. Doctor Generelli could sense Marilyn's nervousness. He looked back and whispered to her. "You'll be fine, Mrs. Leonard."

Reilly led them into a well-appointed living area. The wall between the living room and dining had been opened up as well as the kitchen. It was a nice open plan layout. When the houses were first built all the rooms were separate. Raymond had been seated but stood up as the group entered.

Doctor Generelli said, "Raymond, nice to see you again. I have your mother with me. She's here to visit with you."

Marilyn was almost at a loss from words. It had been so long and now here was her son standing in front of her. *Is this really happening?* she thought, *Do you remember me? You haven't changed much; I would recognize you anywhere.*

"Hello, Raymond. It's so nice to see you. I'm very happy to be here today. Thank you for meeting with me. You look very well, all grown up now."

Raymond didn't say anything at first. He was struggling with the situation and trying to find some words. Then he said, "Hello, mom, I've missed you."

Marilyn's eyes welled up with tears and she had to struggle to not cry. She didn't want to scare Raymond and knew she had to maintain her composure. Doctor Generelli saw that she was not able to speak without breaking down so he took over the conversation.

"It's been a long time for the two of you. Why don't we sit down and catch up on all that's been going on?"

Alastair said, "I have my dog Sherlock with me. This might be a good time for Reilly and me to take her for a walk. She's been in the car for a few hours."

Reilly responded, "Good idea. Raymond are you okay if we go for a walk? We won't be too long. Doctor Generelli will stay with you."

"Okay, I'll be fine."

Sherlock was more than happy to be going for a walk. At the top of the cul-de-sac, there was a walking trail that was once part of a railroad feeder line. It was very popular with the locals. It meandered through a wooded area and was wide enough for both walkers and bikers.

"We have a few of these in Binghamton," said Alastair, "mostly over in Vestal, a village across the river. But this one is the best I've seen."

"I like it and ride my bike on it all the time. Almost nine miles long now with another planned extension next year. Maybe I'll end up riding to Binghamton," laughed Reilly.

The two men and Sherlock ambled along the trail talking about nothing in particular. Alastair knew Reilly was worried about Raymond and the future but did not want to speculate on any outcome at this point. They both would know a lot more later in the day.

"I was surprised when you found me in the police database," said Reilly, "so long ago. Not a happy time in my life. I wasted so many years and for what? Drugs? How stupid could I have been?"

"The good news is it's behind you now and judging from the life you and Raymond have, never coming back. How did you get into running drugs for those guys?"

"I was in my second year at the University of Rochester. I was a recreational user at the time. You know, we all said that to hide our addiction. Recreational use? What a cop-out. You're a druggie, simple as that. One of the dealers offered me the opportunity to pick up and deliver drugs for some good money and also access to much cheaper drug prices. Seemed harmless at the time. I just got in deeper and deeper. In the end, I was making runs all the way to New York City and all-over upstate New York. These guys were violent. If anything went wrong, they would kill you as soon as look at you. A mule is just cheap meat to these guys, especially in the city. Your life has no value. Those guys bragged about the people they killed. There was one guy I dealt with occasionally in the city who actually told me that he killed an FBI agent and his wife. Can you imagine that? He was proud of it."

Alastair stopped walking. He had to catch his breath. *Did I hear that right? What did he just say? An FBI agent and his wife?* Alastair chose his next words very carefully. He did not want to overreact to the comments, but they hit so close to home!

"When was this hit on the FBI guy, did he say?"

"He told me about it about a year or two before I got out of the life. I was in the city picking up some drugs. I think it was something he did a number of years before that. I'd guess it happened maybe ten plus years before."

"Did he say where it happened?"

"Yeah, Miami. He was doing a hit job for someone."

"Did he say who?"

"No, and I didn't ask. I was afraid he'd tell me too much and then kill me to keep it safe. I pretended I didn't care and didn't push the conversation."

"Why did he tell you this?"

"Just to impress me on how important he was. A lot of them were like that. In their minds, big time players. I was always very careful to not get close to them. Nothing good would come of it. Violence was always their default position."

"Do you remember the guy's name?"

"Hmm, let me see, it's been a few years. Wait a second. Yeah, it was Rocco."

"Can you remember his last name?"

"I gotta think about it. These guys never used their last names much. Mostly they used street names. His last name was sort of musical though. Oh, Yeah, I remember, Lanza like the opera singer. Rocco Lanza, that's him."

After all the years of living with the death of his wife and child, he was at the point of finding out who killed them. The FBI was never able to close the case. When they broke up the laundering operation in Miami, they tried to find the killer but nobody would give anything up. As the hit was on an FBI agent, they thought the order for the murder came from high up in the organization. The Miami soldiers were not about to give up their bosses. Although, they did nab some major players in Miami, they couldn't flip any of them. The laundering operation was controlled from New York, so the assumption was the order for the hit came from there. Over time, Alastair's case went cold as many of them do. There were always more criminals to chase.

I wonder if Rocco is still alive, thought Alastair, *if he is I'm going to find him. I will find him and won't rest until I do! Right now I want to kill him but what good would that do? I know I can't get a conviction, too much time has passed and there isn't an evidence trail. But I'll find the son of a bitch; I'll look him straight in the eye and make sure he knows that I know he killed my wife and child. I'll follow him for the rest of his days.*

They headed back to the house. They'd been gone almost two hours now. Both men were curious about the meeting and how things went. Of all things, when they went into the house, they heard Marilyn laughing! They looked at each other and smiled. *Can't be bad,* thought Alastair. Sherlock was with them when they entered the house. When the dog saw Raymond, she immediately went over to him wagging her tail.

"Well, Sherlock's found a new friend," said Reilly, "she barely gave me the time of day."

Although the question was on the tip of their tongues, neither Alastair nor Reilly asked how things went. They would hear soon enough from the doctor and from Marilyn on the way back to Binghamton. It was late in the afternoon and Doctor Generelli suggested that they finish for the day.

"Raymond, would it be okay for both your mother and father to come back next week for a visit?" asked the doctor.

"Sure, will you be here, Doctor? Maybe Maria also."

"I'll be here, and I know Maria would love to join us. And I'll bring the pizza!" Although both Reilly and Maria had met Raymond's parents when they first met in Binghamton, they didn't mention it to Raymond. It might confuse the situation.

As they all stood to leave, there was an awkward moment. Marilyn wanted to give her son a hug and maybe even a kiss. She wasn't sure how Raymond would react so they just stood there looking at each other. Then she said, "Raymond, can I give you a hug before I leave?"

"Sure, he said, and moved in closer to his mother. With a hug and a kiss, the bond was once again established.

Alastair asked her to call her husband and let him know about the meeting. "Let me leave you alone for the call. I'm going to take

Sherlock for a quick walk before we head out. I'm sure she needs a pit stop."

When he got back to the car, he could see that Marilyn had been crying. "Good tears, I bet," said Alastair.

"The best," she replied.

The ride back was surprisingly quiet. So different from the trip to Victor earlier in the day. Marilyn was spent. With the chemo and the emotional meeting today, she didn't have much energy left. They talked for about fifteen minutes then Alastair had her recline her seat and rest. She slept on and off on the way back to Binghamton. Alastair spent the time thinking about Rocco Lanza. *Where are you? Are you alive? I'm coming for you!* He couldn't sleep that night and woke up more tired than when he went to bed. *I've got to put this into perspective,* he thought, *I can't live like this. It'll eat me up. I need to speak with someone who can keep me on track. This anger will cause me to do something stupid.*

Alastair had a friend, Marty Fitzgerald, at The Samaritan Counseling Center in Endicott, a village next to Endwell. They had met when he was conducting an investigation a few years back. Although not on a steady basis, they had maintained contact since then. *I'll call her Monday and see if she can put me with someone or maybe even take me on. I need a third party looking at this.* He also decided to call his old boss at the FBI in Miami. Chris Collins was still there in a more senior position. He was number two at the field office now.

Busy week coming, thought Alastair, *lab reports on the explosives will be coming in, I'm chasing down Rocco Lanza, and trying to hook up with a therapist.*

Chapter 26

First thing on Monday, Alastair called Chris Collins in the Miami field office.

"Chris, can you run a name for me?"

"Can do. Is it part of one of your cases?"

"No, I may have found the guy who killed Emi and the baby."

"You're shitting me!"

"No, I stumbled on to it this past weekend. I've been working on a case trying to find a lad who went missing here some years ago. It took us to Rochester. We were trying to find a drug mule who was in Binghamton back then for a drug pickup. We found the guy. During a conversation with him he mentioned that on one of his trips to the city to pick up drugs, one of the guys he met with was bragging about killing an FBI agent and his wife."

"In Miami?"

"Yep. I don't have any proof, just this conversation. I want to run the guy down and see what I can find out."

"I can see if the guy is in our database, but no frontier justice. The law is the law. If you go rogue, both of us are in serious trouble. You have to promise me you won't take the law into your hands."

"I understand, Chris. I think I've already passed through that gate. When I first heard about it, all I could think about was killing him. I realize this isn't the way to go. I promise I will keep my emotions under control."

"Okay, give me a name."

"Rocco Lanza."

"I've heard that name. Give me a minute and let me see what we have. Do you want to hold?"

"Is the Pope Catholic?"

"I know," laughed Chris, "and next you going to ask me if a bear poops in the woods!"

Alastair was on hold for less than five minutes.

"Yeah, he's in the system. Miami cops even busted him a few years back. Couldn't make the case so had to let him go. He lives up in New York City and is actually on probation now. Loan sharking and a guy was beaten up badly. I'll call the probation officer there and see what your boy is up to.",

"Thanks, Chris, I promise again I won't go off the rails."

"Okay, Al, I'll get back to you soon."

Alastair was comfortable with the developments so far and decided to not call Marty Fitzgerald at The Samaritan Center for now. He had committed to Chris to not go rogue and wouldn't let his old boss and himself down. Revenge was not the main issue anymore. *I just want to see this guy and tell him I know what he did to my family. It doesn't solve anything, but it'll give me the closure I need. Maybe I'll talk to Marty when all of this is over.*

Later that morning, a FedEx package arrived with the lab report on the explosives from Mid-Atlantic. It was quite long and detailed. Almost fifty pages of text and diagrams. *Yikes,* thought Alastair, *where do I start. Maybe with a PhD in chemistry!* As he was pondering the mysteries of the lab report, he got a call from Professor McGinn.

"I guess we're both looking at the same report right now."

"We are and it looks like the butler did it," laughed Alastair.

"Let me help you out. Go to page thirty-nine, second paragraph. The mix of chemicals was wrong. What is really strange is that the mix was too hot in some cases and cold in others. The mixing blend was not consistent. It looks as if they have more than a mixing error, I think some of their production mixers are not working properly. Point is, Al, I don't see this as a one-time error. This could still be happening and may have happened before Trevor bought his stuff from them. I've got a call into Trevor's attorney Floyd Gibson to see if his lab report is back yet. Let's see what he has. I also think we need to get with Henry McArdle at Baker, Bright & Colson. We can't let this information sit until the trial. People could get hurt. Maybe Mid-Atlantic already know about the problem and could be working on it or even fixed it. But we can't take that chance."

"Agreed, we'll set up a conference call with Floyd as soon as he has something. I think Floyd will share the results with us but may not participate in a meeting with Mid-Atlantic. After all, we're still suing Trevor at this point," said Alastair.

"Let the attorneys sort that out, Al. I can never really understand those corporate guys! We need to make sure we're out in front of this. Especially if the problem cuts across the whole company. I should hear from Floyd this morning; I'll get back to you."

Alastair and Chantal spent the rest of the morning interviewing a new client. Nothing as interesting as finding Raymond Leonard or chasing Mid-Atlantic. This case was about stalking. They thought Randy would be a good call for this. It would require a lot of surveillance over a month or so, as well as ready access to phone records. Sherlock was with them in the conference room on her cushion in the corner. She loved being around people. Give her the choice of a room with people in it or an empty room and it was a no-brainer. When they finished the meeting, Alastair took Sherlock to the vets for a checkup. They wanted to keep an eye on her given all the injuries she had. As expected, she passed with flying colors! When they got back to the office, there was a call waiting for him from Professor McGinn.

"What's it look like?" asked Alastair.

"It's a lock. Same results. Hot sticks, cold sticks. They also don't think this was a one-off error. Floyd is sending me a copy of the report today. We need to get rolling on Mid-Atlantic as soon as possible."

"Okay, I'll call Henry over at BB&C and set up a meeting. Do you want to come up for it?"

"It's Henry's call. I can easily do it on the phone or one of the virtual platforms. If they want me to join the meeting, assuming one is going to happen, I'll come up to Binghamton or over to Mid-Atlantic. Floyd is also sending his lab report to Henry at the firm."

"Okay, let's see how Henry wants to play this. Do you need anything from me?" asked Alastair.

"No, we're good, keep in touch."

The rest of the afternoon was fairly quiet. *What's going on with Rocco Lanza?* thought Alastair, *Chris should be back to me by now.* He went to his sister's house that evening to have dinner and talk about the upcoming visit by the boys.

"Should we bring in another washer and dryer for their laundry load?" laughed Alastair, "Or just move the visit over to The Jiffy Laundromat. You could serve the meals over there. That way we can use twenty machines at once!"

"Well, smart guy, that does have some charm!" responded his sister.

About that time his phone rang, and he could see it was a Miami area code. "Sorry, Jane, I need to take this." He went into his old office at the house to speak with Chris Collins.

"Rocco's probation officer was in court most of the day. Finally got back to me. Good guy...he went back to his office after work and dug up the information. Your man Rocco is in a hospice in Teaneck, New Jersey."

"You're kidding!" exclaimed Alastair, "that's pretty much the end of the line, I think."

"Yeah, that's right. Rocco's terminal; stage four lung cancer. He's been in hospice about two weeks now. He went into hospice care before his trial ended. He's in bad shape. Probation is keeping any eye on him until he checks out. What are you going to do?"

"I'm going to go to Teaneck. I want to see him and close this out. Just to see him in the bed and know his life is over is enough. I'm not going to try and confront him."

"Okay, he's in the Bright Days Hospice. It's part of Holy Name Hospital in Teaneck. Do you want me to have one of our agents meet you there? I still worry about how this will impact you."

"I'm good, Chris, I promise. I just want to see this guy and know it's over."

When he returned to the kitchen and his sister Jane, she asked, "What was that all about?"

"We found the guy who killed Emi and the baby."

"Oh, my God, what will happen now? Will they arrest him?"

"No, we can't really prove it, but I know he's the guy. He's in a hospice in New Jersey. I'm going to run down there as soon as I can. I want to see him for myself. I have a meeting with your boys at Baker, Bright & Colson tomorrow, I think. After that I'll head down to Teaneck."

"Are you sure you need to do this, Al? You're opening up some deep wounds. You've built a new life; don't put it at risk."

"I understand and I've thought a lot about this since we found the guy. I need to do this. I have to have closure."

Chapter 27

When Alastair got to the office the next day, there was a message from Henry McArdle confirming a video conference with Mid-Atlantic for the early afternoon. Henry was also concerned about both lab reports and did not want to risk any time delay in confronting Mid-Atlantic with the test results. So, a video call was the quickest way forward. Floyd Gibson, Trevor's attorney was not going to participate in the meeting but had forwarded his lab results to Professor McGinn and Henry.

At two o'clock that afternoon, Henry, Alastair, and Professor McGinn were linked into Mid-Atlantic on a Zoom call. There were some new players in the meeting from Mid-Atlantic. Surprisingly, the vice-president of manufacturing was not there. One of the new faces in the meeting was the general manager of the operation.

Henry McArdle opened the meeting. "Gentlemen, thank you for meeting with us on such short notice. I realize this is rather unusual, but information has come to our attention that we feel duty-bound to pass on to you immediately, and not wait for a trial. We had Brigham Analytics near Boston do an analysis of four of the dynamite sticks purchased from your company by Trevor Durgan. Floyd Gibson, who represents Trevor, also had four units tested by another lab near Philadelphia. Their name is Filmont Labs. Both laboratories reported identical findings. The test results indicate that the explosives in question may not be a one-off situation, but are indicative of a continuing problem with your manufacturing process and equipment. If that's the case, we felt you should be made aware of the situation as soon as possible. This may be an ongoing situation and demands your immediate attention.

Nobody responded immediately. Alastair wished they were meeting in person so it would be easier to read the body language of Mid-Atlantic. After some minutes, the general manager of Mid-Atlantic, Barry Altmore, advised that they were going to another room to meet off-camera and asked that the Baker, Bright & Colson team remain on the call.

When they left the room, Henry and Alastair called Professor McGinn on a separate phone line. "I don't think we told them anything new," said Henry, "we probably confirmed their thinking or maybe even their test results assuming they also ran some testing."

"I agree," said Professor McGinn, "nobody fell off their chairs. Just grim faces hearing what they already know."

"Looks that way," said Alastair, "what are the next steps? We have an open case pending."

Henry replied, "they'd be foolish to go to trial. The evidence is overwhelming. My sense is that they will look hard at their liability insurance policies and settle. Also, submit a full disclosure to the State of Pennsylvania about the problem and how they've rectified it. If they try to hide this, they could lose everything. Let's see what they have to say, they should be back shortly."

When the Mid-Atlantic team rejoined the meeting, their general manager thanked the Binghamton team for the information and asked for copies of the lab reports. The meeting was pretty much finished at that point. There wasn't anything more to discuss. Mid-Atlantic knew they were the ones with the problem and had to make the next move.

Henry McArdle summarized Baker, Bright Colson's position. "Mr. Altmore, we have an ongoing case against Mid-Atlantic and will continue to pursue it unless we hear differently from you. Our plan is to prepare for trial."

"Certainly, Mr. McArdle, I understand your position. I can't comment further at this time. I need to meet with our president and most likely the board of directors. I'll be back to you as this develops."

With that, the meeting ended. Henry asked Professor McGinn to stay on the call. The Mid-Atlantic team had left the meeting. "I'm going to call Floyd Gibson this afternoon and tell him we're dropping the case against Trevor. No sense dragging them though any of this. He may even want to take action against Mid-Atlantic for selling Trevor a defective product."

"Well," laughed Alastair, "you could represent Trevor in a new case!"

"Hmm, I think Floyd's firm in Philadelphia has a stable full of hard chargers who can run with this. I'd hate to be Mid-Atlantic," replied Henry.

When Henry called Floyd to tell him they were dropping the suit against Trevor, he caught him just coming back from court. "Thanks, Henry, this has been hard on Trevor. He's never been down this road before. Liability is always a worry for someone in Trevor's line of work. He'll be so happy to get the news. When I was with Trevor in the Army doing demolition work, he was always the guy who kept the rest of us cowboys in line. He was pragmatic and cautious. He always said you have to respect this stuff, or it'll kill you. I always felt he couldn't be at fault. Now we have the evidence."

"Are you going to go after Mid-Atlantic?"

"I'm going to pass the case over to a colleague in the firm who does this kind of litigation. He'll make the call. We may want a co-counsel up in the Binghamton area. Interested?"

"Always."

"Okay, we'll be in touch."

The ball was in Mid-Atlantic's court.

Chapter 28

The next morning, bright and early, Alastair was on his way to Teaneck, New Jersey. As always with these kinds of road trips, a travel mug of coffee and a multi-grain bagel from Price Chopper with peanut butter. The breakfast of road warriors! He took route seventeen through the Catskills then past Bear Mountain. Much better scenery than the interstate, and he wanted some more time to think about meeting Rocco Lanza. He made an early start as he planned to make the trip in one day. His nephews were coming for the weekend, and he wanted to be back for dinner. Jane would be making Shephard's Pie, a family favorite!

He arrived in Teaneck a little after ten-thirty, parked the car in the big hospital parking lot, and went to the hospice located next to the hospital. He told the receptionist that he was there to see Rocco Lanza. She directed him to the nurse's station on the second floor.

"Are you family?" asked the duty nurse.

"Not really, we were both in a situation in Miami awhile back when I was with the FBI. How is Rocco doing?"

When he said FBI, the nurse seemed to put him in a different category. Not family for sure but maybe someone who Rocco would want to see. "I'm afraid he's declining. We see a marked difference from last week. He sleeps a lot these days. You can look into his room, maybe he's awake. If he's sleeping, please don't disturb him. He's on heavy medications now and rest is important. It's room two-twenty-six.

Alastair went to Rocco's room and stood outside, reading the card on the wall with the name of the patient. Rocco Lanza. A life of violence and murder and then you end up in a hospice with stage four lung cancer. Maybe this is some form of justice. But what about the other folks who try to live a good life and end up in the same place. *I'll never understand this,* thought Alastair, *none of this seems to fit. My wife and baby dead, and the murderer here in a hospice. Go figure that out!*

"Are you here to see my grandpa?" asked a young woman with dark hair and a beautiful smile. "I'm on my way to my classes at Fairleigh-Dickson University. I try to stop by and see Grandpa as often as I can. He's fading now and there's not many days left."

They stepped into the room and looked at the small, frail man in the bed. So thin and curled up in a fetal position. Alastair looked over her shoulder and was surprised at the condition of Rocco. *Are you the guy who murdered Emi and the baby? I expected somebody much bigger.* Rocco was sleeping and they didn't want to disturb him. The young woman went over to a small table with two chairs in the corner of the room.

"We can sit here for a bit," she said, "maybe grandpa will wake up. He never gets any visitors; he'll be happy to see you."

Alastair didn't want to sit in the room but he could not refuse the young girl. So innocent and clearly attached to her grandpa. "How do you know Grandpa?"

"Oh, we go back to Miami a number of years ago." said Alastair.

"I know he used to go there on business," she said, "he always brought me back presents. I still have some of them in my room at home. Silly things, looking at them now, but I still like them."

As awkward as it was sitting there talking with his granddaughter, it was compelling. Here was a guy dying in the bed next to them and the young girl had such fond memories of him. Rocco Lanza, murderer, loan shark and enforcer. None of this makes any sense. She recounted birthdays and holidays with her grandpa and all Alastair could think about was this man killed my wife and baby.

This is surreal, he thought, *you can't write this stuff.* They sat there for about twenty minutes then decided that they best leave Rocco alone to rest. As they were getting up to leave, Rocco opened his eyes and saw them. He was groggy from the drugs and sleep but recognized his granddaughter. She came over to his bed to talk with him. Alastair stayed in the background. As the two talked she said, "Grandpa, there is a man who knows you from Miami. I met him in the hall. She motioned for Alastair to come over to the bed. When he got there Rocco starred at him intently. It was hard to tell if he knew or remembered him after all these years. But Rocco wouldn't take his eyes off him.

Rocco was clearly tired and starting to fade. He wouldn't stay awake much longer. Alastair leaned close to Rocco and said, "I was in the area and wanted to stop by and say hello. You met my wife and me in Miami when I was with the FBI. You were down there on a contract. Nice to have found you."

At that point, Alastair knew he remembered. His facial expression didn't change dramatically but he could see it in his eyes and hear it in his breathing. Rapid eye movement and a decided shortness of breath. The nurse came by on her rounds and put Rocco back on oxygen. His granddaughter said goodbye and they left the room. As they walked out of the building together, she said, "Thank you for visiting my grandpa. I'm sure he appreciated it."

"I hope so," said Alastair, "it's been a long time. Good luck to you at school. Promise me you won't get married until you're twenty-five and successful!"

"Wow, you sound just like my father.!"

The ride back to Binghamton was fairly easy. He left Teaneck ahead of the afternoon traffic. He was back at his sister's house in plenty of time to sit and talk about the day and have a Ballantine's scotch and soda. The boys had arrived but were out with their friends. All of them telling each other tall tales of romance with the ladies and speculating on the upcoming season for the Buffalo Bills.

His sister said, "Al, looks like you found some closure. You were really wound up the other day."

"I did, sis. When I went to the hospice, I had no idea how it would play out. The guy is close to death and I'm happy I was able to go there and see him. He remembered Emi and me. By the way, I met his granddaughter, sweet kid. So, maybe there's hope for us after all."

He took a few minutes to call Chris Collins at the FBI office in Miami to fill him in on the visit and thank him for his help.

"I saw him and I know he remembered me, Chris. He only has a few days left. Finally, I found closure. This has finally come full circle. By the way, I'm going to be in Miami soon. I want to visit Emi's grave and see her parents. I want to tell them about Rocco. I'll give you a call when I head down. Find some time and we can go to the International Grille and tell each other lies! Hell, I'll even pay the bill!

"Then I'm available!" laughed Chris.

After the call, Alastair took Sherlock for a walk in the dog park nearby. It was always busy this time of day. Folks home from work and taking their dogs out for some exercise. Although he didn't know many by name, they recognized each other from previous visits with their dogs. There were always groups sitting around on the benches. Nice, pleasant conversations, free from politics and religion. Just simple talk about the weather and their dogs. I don't care about your religion or your politics but I do care about your dog and how you're doing. How good is that during these times?

Chapter 29

Dinner with the boys was always fun. The animated conversations and energy were a tonic for him especially after the last few weeks. Between the quarry accident investigation, Raymond Leonard, and Rocco Lanza it had been a roller coaster ride. As for Rocco it was over. Not much left to think about. Rocco would be gone in a matter of days and never back in Alastair's life. However, there were still a number of open items left dealing with Raymond and the quarry accident.

This was pretty much Doctor Generelli's show now regarding Raymond. The challenge was to integrate him back into his family and maintain his life in Rochester. Alastair felt the prospects for a successful conclusion were quite good. The elephant in the room was whether or not Raymond would be able to finally deal with the trauma of the murders in Binghamton. However, Doctor Generelli had wisely kept the reunification with his family and murders in Binghamton in separate boxes. Alastair made two calls that evening. The first was to Doctor Generelli to let him know he was ready to provide whatever support was needed. The two men agreed to stay in touch as Raymond's therapy unfolded. The second call was to Marilyn Leonard.

"Marilyn, just checking in with you to see how it's going and to let you know you can call me anytime if you need my help. You're off the books now. This is from one friend to another."

"Oh, Al, thank you so much. We seem to be moving along pretty well. Hubert and I were with Raymond the other week and had a great visit. Doctor Generelli wants us to keep meeting a couple of times a month for now. He's also seeing Raymond once a week. He's doesn't talk about the sessions other than go give me a top-level overview. I think he's satisfied with the progress. I don't know if they're talking about the murders yet. Reilly and Maria have been great. I really like them. I'm so happy with everything. I don't even think about my cancer anymore. The doctors are happy with my chemo treatments. What else can an old lady ask for!"

The quarry accident was not resolved at this point. Mid-Atlantic had yet to step up and do the right thing. Professor McGinn and Alastair were sure that the problem was much more than a one-off mistake. Most likely, more serious, cutting across their total manufacturing process. Baker, Bright & Colson had advised them of the lab results from both testing firms. Now it was up to Mid-Atlantic to take the next steps. Alastair thought they would certainly want to settle out of court, but stranger things have happened in cases like this. All they could do is wait for Mid-Atlantic to play the next round of cards and prepare for trial.

In the meantime, Alastair set about cleaning up some small cases, or odd-jobs as Chantal called them, that were still open and get the insurance fraud case moving. He would need Randy to do a lot of legwork on this case. Surveillance for sure and extensive interviews. This was not a case of a one-time claim; it had a long history spanning almost nine years.

Alastair could see a bit of a window in the upcoming week and decided to visit Emi's parents in Florida. They were not yet aware that Alastair had found the killer, let alone met him. He didn't want to have this conversation over the phone. Emi's parents, Nigel and Marie, were happy for the opportunity to meet as it had been almost a year since they last were together. He made arrangements for Chantal to look after Sherlock for a few days and called Emi's parents.

"I have some news about the guy who killed Emi and the baby," said Alastair, "can I come down to Fort Walton Beach and talk about it when we meet?"

"After all these years? I can't believe it! Good news?" asked Nigel.

"It is."

"We've missed you, my boy; it'll be great to see you again."

It took two connecting flights to get from Binghamton to Fort Walton Beach. The weather was good and the flight connections were pretty much on time. Nigel met him at the airport.

"Look at you," said Nigel, "you look great. I'm just an old fart in the departure lounge waiting for the call!"

"You're full of it, Nigel," laughed Alastair, "you don't show your age at all. I bet you have at least a week left before you check out!"

"We're both doing well, Al. Day at a time as you can imagine but we're lucky. We both work hard on our exercise routines and have a nice social life. I can't complain but I guess I do. Don't listen to me!"

It was late in the afternoon when they arrived at the house. Marie had prepared a cheese board, olives, and a selection of nuts. Dinner would come later in the evening.

"I have some Ballantine's, Al. Half scotch, half soda in a large Old-Fashioned glass?" asked Nigel.

"You got it, thanks."

Marie joined the men for cocktails. She had a glass of chilled Sancerre. A white wine that could be well chilled without losing its taste. Earnest Hemingway was right! Nigel was always a scotch drinker and had settled on Ballantine's years ago when he first met Alastair. They sat in the Lanai. There was a mild breeze off the Gulf providing a welcome change of air. Their house faced south giving them a nice view of the gulf.

"Always nice to be here with you," said Alastair, "I've always liked this house. I know you're eager to hear the news about the guy who killed Emi and the baby. I need to take a few steps back to have this make any sense, so bear with me. I've been working on a case involving a young lad in Binghamton who witnessed a double homicide a number of years ago. It was robbery or drug deal gone bad. He's autistic and was traumatized by the killings. The killer saw him and tried to kill him also. He ran away and ended up in Rochester, New York. He attached himself to a guy at the bus terminal who was actually in Binghamton to bring the drugs back to Rochester."

"Do you mean they were both witnesses to the same murder?" asked Marie.

"Not quite. The drug mule, that's the guy who was there to bring the drugs back to Rochester, came onto the scene after the murders. He saw the bodies and ran away before the police arrived. The young lad, whose name is Raymond, actually witnessed the killings. He also ran away. The two of them connected at the bus terminal. Raymond had completely blocked all memories of the murders from his mind. The drug mule knew that it was a drug deal gone bad or a robbery but that's all."

"Did he know Raymond had witnessed the murders?"

"No, as I mentioned, the lad had blocked it all from his memory. All the drug mule knew was that Raymond was traumatized by something and at a loss about where to go."

"Are you kidding me?" exclaimed Marie.

"No, it really happened. The drug mule, whose name is Reilly, took Raymond in and cared for him and got out of the drug life. They've lived together now for close to ten years. When we found Raymond in Rochester, I brought his mother over to meet her son. Reilly's longtime girlfriend Maria insisted that a therapist be involved. It was quite complicated. He was still traumatized by the murders and had been away from his parents for almost ten years. During one of my trips to Rochester, I spent some time with Reilly while the therapist, Raymond, and his mother were reconnecting. Reilly and I were talking about the violence of the drug life and how you can't last very long in it before you end up in jail or dead. He mentioned that on one of his drug trips to New York City, one of the men he usually met there bragged that he killed an FBI agent and his wife in Miami."

"Oh, my God!" said Nigel.

"Apparently, he didn't know I survived. Probably didn't matter to them. They sent their message to us and that was the main point. I was able to find the guy in the FBI database. His name is Rocco Lanza. Turns out he's on probation and in a hospice in Teaneck, New Jersey with stage four lung cancer. He has but a few days left. I went to the hospice last week and saw him. He is heavily sedated and sleeps most of the time. I didn't have a conversation with him. But, when I left, I leaned over and told him Emi and I met him in Miami during my FBI days. He remembered us and knew I found him."

"What happens now?" asked Marie.

"Nothing, he'll be dead in a few days. But at least I know who committed the murders and was able to confront him. I finally have a sense of closure."

"Oh, Al," said Marie, "you poor guy, having to go through all of this yet again. Are you going to be okay?"

"I am now. It's finally come full circle."

The next morning, he borrowed Nigel's car and went to the cemetery to visit Emi and the baby. Nigel and Marie felt he wanted to be alone and stayed behind. When he arrived at the cemetery there was a new grave near to Emi's. The ground above the grave had not settled and a headstone had not been placed there yet. He went up and stood by his wife's grave. *My sweet Emi, the years will never dull the pain of not having you and the baby with me. I have a new life now and it's been good, but it will never replace you and the baby. I miss you so much. Even though I've found the killer, it doesn't make up for what he did. But he'll be gone soon and can never hurt anyone again.*

As he was standing there, he felt the presence of someone nearby. He looked around and noticed an elderly man standing near the new grave. The made eye contact and Alastair nodded to the man. The man nodded back and walked over to Alastair.

"It's comforting to see someone visiting the final resting place of a loved one. Do you visit often?"

"I live in New York now and try to come at least once a year. My wife's parents live nearby, and we've kept in touch over the years."

"My wife just died. We were married over fifty years."

"That's a big loss, takes time to sort it all out. Be patient and take it a step at a time."

"How long has it been for you?"

"My wife died over twelve years ago. Over time you can sort of put it all in perspective and continue to live your life. Not the same as before. You have to build a new one."

The two men stood there for some minutes, neither speaking. Both thinking of days gone by. Sometimes, communication is more effective without words.

"Well, it was nice to meet you, sir. Thanks for your time and the thoughtful words," said the man.

"Good luck, my friend," replied Alastair, "trust me, you have good days ahead of you."

Alastair went back to the car to head back to Marie and Nigel's house. He didn't start driving right away. He sat in the car thinking about his days with Emi and the recent events regarding Rocco Lanza. After an hour, he drove slowly out of the cemetery. The next day he took a flight to Miami to meet Chris Collins. They met at the International Grille for dinner. Always good food and service. Surprisingly, they didn't talk much about the old days. Chris was quite interested in the meeting with Rocco. They spent time talking about it and how the case was never closed by the FBI. They put a lot of time and effort into finding Emi's killer but could not never solve it.

"I'm really happy for you, Al. Finally able to confront the killer. It always bothered me. We knew who set it up but could not tie anyone to the killing. I've let the bureau know that you found Rocco. I don't think they'll take any action at this point. The guy's well on his way out. They'll stay in touch with the New York City probation office and keep an eye on the hospice just to make sure it all ends there."

After that, the conversation was mostly about family, friends, and the future. Chris had turned down two promotions which would have meant moving the family. The kids were doing great in school and Chris and his wife Darlene didn't want to disrupt them. This meant he had pretty much capped his career with the FBI. His kids were in college now and he would retire in less than five years.

So, Al, what am I going to do when I grow up? I'm running out of time! All I see ahead are hard decisions. Do we stay here or go back to Maine? Where will the kids end up? Nothing is clear at this point."

"Give it some time, Chris. These things have a way of presenting you with the obvious solution. Having never remarried, my sister and her boys in Endwell are very important to me. They live nearby and her boys have adopted me. She's been divorced longer than I've been alone so we all have bonded together. I love my life. My point is that you and Darlene will sort it all out and in the end your decisions will make good sense. I'm not trying to dismiss this, Chris. You guys will end up in a good place. I promise."

"You're right, I know that; but I do worry and think about it a lot these days."

"Just think about it, don't worry about it. Anyway, here come our steaks, let's deal with the important things!"

The next day Alastair was on an early morning flight to Atlanta, a connection to Syracuse and then a drive south to Binghamton. There wasn't a direct flight to Syracuse until later in the day.

Chapter 30

When he arrived in Binghamton, he drove over to Chantal's house to pick up Sherlock. As he entered the house, he called out to Sherlock who was with the boys in the basement. The dog responded with a limp woof!

"Wow, didn't she miss me just a bit?" laughed Alastair.

"You've got some competition from the boys, Al; you have to up your game!"

Alastair and Chantal spoke briefly about the upcoming week at the agency. The insurance case was a going forward. They had received a retainer from the company and would start it as soon as Randy was available, no later than mid-week. Chantal would also be needed for some of the surveillance which was very interesting for her. She had done a fair amount of surveillance on past cases with good results. Alastair was starting to think about having her work full-time on investigations. He needed more boots on the ground; the business was growing. Randy was always available but being an independent consultant and investigator, sometimes you had to wait until he could free himself up.

Chantal liked the prospect of working outside of the office. Sometimes the walls could close in on you. There were also two other calls during the week regarding new investigations; Chantal expected both of them to move forward.

"Was there any word from Baker, Bright & Colson on the quarry accident case?" asked Alastair.

"Nothing this week. Professor McGinn called asking if we heard anything and I told him no news so far. What do you think?"

"Oh, I guess wheels are turning there. If Mid-Atlantic have to get in front of their president and board, it usually takes a bit of time to get all their ducks lined up. Maybe this week?"

Shortly after Alastair and Sherlock arrived at the office the next day, Doctor Generelli called. "Al, I want to come over to Binghamton next weekend. I'll have Raymond and Reilly with me. He's making good progress. I want him to visit his parents at their house. It'll be a one-day visit. I think he's ready to see where he grew up. I wonder if you can join us? You've been instrumental in finding Raymond and his parents trust you.

"I'd be happy to, Doc. Just let me know what time."

"Mid-morning, I think. I'll call you when I'm close. By the way, can you bring your dog? It's Sherlock, isn't it? Raymond quite likes her and has mentioned her a number of times during our sessions."

"Sure. See you soon."

Raymond was not at all apprehensive about the upcoming visit. However, Reilly was worried. He was afraid that Raymond would want to visit the site of the murders and the effect it might have on him. Doctor Generelli was aware of the risk and assured Reilly that it would not happen. If the murder site came up in the conversation, he would tell Raymond that it was for another day. He told Reilly he didn't think it would come up but if it did, he would handle it.

So on Saturday, they were off to Binghamton. Reilly driving, Raymond in the passenger side front seat and the doctor in the back seat. The conversation between Reilly and Raymond was mostly on upgrading the office software. The current system was cumbersome in terms of coding the patient services into the Medicaid and Medicare systems.

"We need a new system that will be periodically updated," said Reilly, "our current one is way out of date and no way now to upgrade it."

"You're right," said Raymond, "I'm spending a lot of time at the end of each day trying to get the systems to talk to each other. Let's get some companies in and see what they have. I've read up on a system called Medi-Master and like it. We can start with them."

"Alright, let's get it started," said Reilly.

This is quite interesting, thought the doctor, *no signs of apprehension about the visit. It's almost like a social outing for them. Raymond seems to be going from strength to strength. We may be pretty close to opening up the murders he witnessed. He's very secure with Reilly and now with his parents. I don't want to get ahead of the progress but I don't think we could've written a better scenario.*

Alastair and Sherlock were waiting for them when they arrived. As before, Sherlock bounded up to Raymond, tail wagging. She followed him into the house. His mother was worried that he may find the house unsettling, but he happily walked around the house looking in all the rooms with Sherlock at his side.

"Let's leave him to explore along with Sherlock. He seems quite comfortable," said Doctor Generelli.

While Raymond was off on his exploration adventure, the others sat in the kitchen having coffee and Danish. For lunch, Raymond's mother had prepared some of his favorite dishes. She hoped it would help him be more comfortable in the house. When he returned he joined the group in the kitchen and asked for a cup of coffee.

"My, you were never a coffee drinker when you were here," laughed his mother.

"Reilly got me started. He's always drinking coffee. Now I'm sort of the same way."

"Not to worry, Mrs. Leonard, I stopped drinking alcohol years ago," Reilly said to a loud round of laughs.

"Mom, the house is very nice, just like I remember it," said Raymond, "it even smells the same."

"I'm glad you like it. You and Reilly can come back anytime to visit. I know you have a home and a life in Rochester, but you can always come visit dad and me."

"We'd like that," said Reilly.

Raymond and Reilly, along with Sherlock, decided to take a short walk around the neighborhood. A lot had changed over the years. New neighbors, house colors and new additions to some of them. They didn't go more than a couple of blocks from the house. It was a good first step for Raymond on his road back. When they returned, Mrs. Leonard had prepared a cold lunch of deli-meats and salad. Included was ham salad from Weis' Super Market, one of Raymond's favorite dishes. Desert was also a favorite, brownies! After lunch, they sat around talking about upstate New York and the changes happening around the State. About three, they decided to leave and head back to Rochester. Again, a very successful visit.

I'm going to start opening up the murders, thought Doctor Generelli, *we're at a good place now. Raymond feels secure. I think we can take the next steps. I'm going to see him next Thursday. I'll start to put it on the table.*

After they left to go back to Rochester, Alastair and Sherlock stayed for a few minutes more. Marilyn wanted to talk.

"Al, what do you think about trying to get Raymond to deal with those murders? He seems so happy now. Do we need to expose him to all that trauma from years ago?"

"It's the doc's call, Marilyn, but I think he has to deal with it or never really make a full recovery. You have to trust Doctor Generelli. I do."

Hubert said, "I'm sure you're right, Al. We just don't want to lose the gains we've made. He's been gone for so long and now he's back. We don't want to lose him again."

"I know the doc is aware of the risks. He took care to make sure the reunion with you and the murders were kept separate. I think he can try to get Raymond to deal with the murders now and not risk his relationship with you and Marilyn."

"I'm still worried," said Marilyn.

"That's a mother's job," replied Alastair

Chapter 31

The next day Alastair was at the office talking with Randy on the phone about the upcoming insurance fraud investigation when Chantal poked her head into the office.

"Al, Henry McArdle from Baker, Bright & Colson is on the other line. Can you take the call?"

"Sure. Randy let me come back to you, I need to take another call. Back to you shortly."

"Al, this is Henry McArdle, we got a call from Mid-Atlantic. They want to meet day after tomorrow at our offices. Can you make it?"

"Sure, what about Professor McGinn?"

"I'll call him when we finish."

"Do you think they're going to offer a settlement?"

"Yeah, if they were going to continue the case, they wouldn't have contacted us. I don't know what they want to put on the table. They only asked for a meeting. We've discussed it within the firm and know where we want to go. Let's see what plays out with Mid-Atlantic."

"What about Trevor Durgan's attorney. Will he be there?"

"No, we don't have a case pending against Trevor now. We dropped it. His attorney, Floyd Gibson, may well try to go after Mid-Atlantic as they apparently sold Trevor a compromised product and put him as risk. It's their call on what they choose to do."

When they met with Mid-Atlantic, the tone of the meeting had changed from the earlier meetings. They had a problem and everyone knew it now. Mid-Atlantic was represented by their general manager, vice president of quality control, and two attorneys. One from the company and another from a law firm in Scranton. Henry settled everyone into the meeting and said, "Okay, gentlemen, what do you want to do?"

Barry Altmore, the general manager, opened the meeting. "Gentlemen, thanks for the meeting on such short notice. Let me be very candid with you. Our lab tests confirmed your findings. Our manufacturing process was compromised. We've fixed it and have notified all our customers about the problem, especially the ones who may have been impacted directly. I believe we have recovered and destroyed all the product in question. We'd like to settle with your clients now."

"What are your thoughts on a settlement offer?" asked Henry.

"We will certainly cover all their medical expenses. Additionally, compensate all five of your clients."

"What is your compensation offer?" asked Henry.

"Two of the quarrymen were hurt seriously and three received only minor injuries. I realize that there was an element of trauma and we recognize this. We are prepared to offer the two men who were seriously injured five-hundred thousand dollars each. We'll pay the three other quarrymen two-hundred thousand each. Additionally, we'll cover the medical expenses for all five men."

"Barry, give us a few minutes to talk among ourselves."

The Binghamton team went to another meeting room to discuss the offer.

"I'm no expert on settlement offers, but this seems quite reasonable," said Alastair.

"I'm surprised," said Henry, "it is much better than I expected. Maybe they just want to settle and get on with their business."

"Are you going to accept it?" asked Professor McGinn.

"Sort of," said Henry, "it's along the lines of what we discussed among ourselves the other day. I want to make a few changes but on balance, I think it's acceptable. Ultimately, the quarrymen will make the call. It's their decision. I don't see getting into long-protracted negotiations with Mid-Atlantic. They've cleaned up their house and appear to be on solid footing now that they fixed their problem. So, they really don't have an overriding incentive to settle quickly anymore. If they want to play hardball, they could string this out, but I don't think they want to do this. They want to close the case and the offer supports their position of closing this out."

When they went back into the meeting room, Henry spoke. "Barry, I have a couple of changes for your team to consider. As I remember, all the quarrymen are being cared for by The Geisinger Clinic in Scranton. I want them to be covered for ten years in case there are lingering issues. I'm comfortable with Geisinger. They are ethical and I don't see any risk of any potential future claims being abused. I'm willing to have you stipulate that Geisinger will provide the primary and follow-up care for the men. I want to increase the settlements. One of the quarrymen is still out of work and may not ever be able to return. He suffered a significant head injury. I'm proposing an eight-hundred-thousand-dollar settlement for him. The other man is out of the hospital and recovering. I'm proposing a six-hundred-thousand-dollar settlement for him. For the remaining three quarrymen, I'm proposing two-hundred-fifty thousand dollars. Admittedly, they were not seriously injured but they were struck by debris and required medical attention."

"Okay, Henry, let us talk among ourselves," said Barry.

As they waited in the other conference room, Professor McGinn asked, "Henry, I guess you're not a betting man, but what do you think?"

"They should take it, it's a reasonable counteroffer. I don't want to get into any mind-numbing negotiations, and I think Barry feels the same way. Now that they've sorted out their company, I think they want to put all this behind them."

After not too long a time, the Mid-Atlantic company attorney asked the Binghamton team to join them back in the conference room. There was no apparent hostility from Mid-Atlantic. Barry Altmore was clearly in charge of the Mid-Atlantic group.

"Henry, we can accept your counteroffer. I think we both feel the same way. Time to settle and move on. I'm not of the mind to try and incorporate any statements about not admitting wrongdoing or not disclosing the settlement value to third parties. Our customer base is relatively small. Some of them have been with us for years. I want the settlement to be clear. We had a problem. We fixed it. We compensated the injured parties."

"I agree. Let's leave the attorneys alone to write this up. I'll have lunch brought in so we can finish this up. We'll put the attorneys in the other conference room, and we can have lunch brought in here."

Barry laughed, "No lunch for the lawyers until they have a draft for us to review!"

The final agreement was finished in the early afternoon. Henry had to review the proposed settlement with his clients but did not expect any issues with their acceptance.

"I'll meet with my clients soon and call you. I expect it will be late this week or early next week. I'll call you and follow up with a formal letter."

After the Mid-Atlantic group left, the three men sat in the conference room discussing the meeting and the outcome. Everyone was happy with the proposed settlement and expected the quarrymen to accept it.

Professor McGinn had seen a different slice of life working on this case. So different from the classroom. "I'm going to make a project out of this for my senior seminar," he said, "this will give the students a great insight into how their education and technology plays out in the real world. I'm always getting pushback from them on the relevancy of some of their courses. Now I have a great example to talk about and I was part of the team."

Alastair asked, "What do you think Trevor and Floyd will do? It looks like they have a case against Mid-Atlantic."

"Well, they do...and they don't," said Henry, "Trevor was not injured and he was cleared of any wrongdoing. So, I don't see any material damage. However, he was put at significant risk. He was closest to the explosion. Fortunately, it didn't blow out in his direction. If it did, we'd be having a much different conversation. But he was at risk and is a long-time customer. Also, his reputation is at risk. On balance, it's all worth something. So, I expect they'll make some kind of offer to him. In the meantime, let's speak with the quarrymen."

Chapter 32

Doctor Generelli typically met with Raymond at the Evercare office in Victor. It was an easy trip for him, and he liked meeting with Raymond in familiar surroundings. Sometimes patients were intimidated by a location. Reilly was usually out on a case when they met and would stop by after he finished to pick up Raymond. They usually started the session with Raymond telling the doctor about the previous week. Any issues? Any problems? From there, the doctor would take the lead.

Today the doctor opened their session on a different note asking, "I want to talk about something that happened to you a long time ago and caused you a lot of pain and worry. Can we try to do this?"

"I guess, but do we have to?"

"We do. It's important to understand what happened to you so you can get well. I know this has been with you for a long time now. We need to put it on the table. You'll always be safe. Reilly and Maria are with you here in Victor and your mother and father in Binghamton. Nobody can hurt you."

Raymond sat for some minutes thinking about all that was said. He would have dreams about that bad time but had never been able to see it all. Only patches of it in his dreams.

"Once you start to talk about this Raymond, more will come back. It may make you uncomfortable or scared but I'm here with you and will guide you through it. You can do this."

Raymond was silent again and then spoke. "I remember the bad man chasing me with a gun. He was trying to hurt me."

"Did he yell at you or talk to you?"

"He told me to stop running but I wasn't going to do that. He wanted to hurt me."

"Why was he chasing you?"

"I saw some really bad things."

"Can you tell me what you saw."

Raymond did not respond immediately. He was clearly disturbed and reliving the whole experience, yet again. Doctor Generelli did not try to take him any further into the trauma. He sat quietly waiting for Raymond to speak. After some minutes, he gently spoke to him.

"It's okay, Raymond, you're safe, nobody can hurt you."

Raymond responded, "I saw him shoot some men. They were yelling at each other and then he just shot them. They fell on the ground and he shot them again. I saw him do it. I saw it all. Then he saw me and ran after me."

"Okay, Raymond, what else can you remember?"

"I ran to the bus station to get away. Reilly found me and helped me."

He had finally arrived at the point where he remembered that awful time and could talk about it. Locked in his mind for years and now out in the open. It was a relief.

"Why couldn't I remember it all before?"

"It's quite common. We block bad things out of our minds because they scare us or are too painful to deal with," said the doctor, "you did nothing wrong. You were protecting yourself. You were also trying to protect your mother and father by staying away from them all these years. You were afraid the bad man would find them and hurt them, too."

Once Raymond started to understand the reasons for his actions, he felt much calmer and was more willing to talk about the murders.

He realized he was not in danger and more importantly, had not done anything wrong. The doctor felt he had taken it as far as he could safely do for the day. They agreed to meet the following week. He asked him to think about visiting his mother and father soon and maybe walking by the old lots where the murders happened.

"You don't have to do this, but I think it will give you the chance to close out this terrible chapter once and for all."

"Will you come to Binghamton? Reilly, too?"

"Sure, we will, and we can walk along with you if you want us to."

"Can I see Sherlock while we're there?"

"Always," laughed the doctor.

The next week Raymond and the doctor met at the Evercare office. Reilly had just returned from a visit with a home care patient. Doctor Generelli asked him to join them. He felt it was important for Reilly to hear the whole story. He may have put some of the pieces together over the years, but it was important to hear everything. Raymond continued to remember more of that awful day and was now able to tell Reilly a complete story.

When Raymond finished telling him about the murders, Reilly said, "Wow, I didn't know it was so bad. Thank you for telling me about it. You never have to worry about this again, it's over, all over."

The following week, Raymond, Reilly, and Doctor Generelli were off to Binghamton to meet up with Raymond's' parents and go to the lot where Raymond witnessed the murders. When they arrived at his parent's house, Alastair was already there along with Sherlock. When the dog saw Raymond, she bounded over to him, her tail wagging.

"Reilly, you guys need to get a dog," laughed Alastair, "Raymond's a natural."

"I've been thinking about that. Maybe a rescue dog. About the size of Sherlock with a good temperament."

Alastair and the Leonards stayed behind while Raymond, Reilly and Doctor Generelli along with Sherlock went to the lot where the murders happened so many years ago. Raymond insisted that Sherlock join them. The murder scene was about five blocks from the Leonard's house. Since the murders, two small houses had been built on the lots by Habitat for Humanity. As they got closer, Raymond slowed down. Maybe trying to recognize old landmarks or just nervous about what was next. When they arrived at the lots, Raymond looked in, deep in his thoughts.

He looked between the houses and said to Reilly, "The bad man shot them right over there, pointing to a plastic toy between the houses, left in the yard by a young child. It's different now with the houses but I saw it happen, right there."

It seemed to the doctor that this was almost a non-event. The trauma was mostly gone and it was almost as if they were on a guided tour or a trip down memory lane. Going back to the scene of the crime so to say, was interesting to Raymond but not a profound experience. Clearly, he had finally arrived at the point where he could deal with the past.

When they returned to the house, Reilly and Raymond continued to walk through the neighborhood, taking Sherlock with them. This gave the doctor a chance to brief the Leonards and Alastair on the visit to the murder scene.

"I think we've taken this as far as we can. Your son has addressed all the issues from the past and frankly, has moved on. I don't think we need to do anything more at this point. He's in a good place psychologically speaking. Keep the visits going; Rochester and here. Take your lead from Reilly and Raymond. They may want to come down and stay overnight. Same for you going over there. Make some days out of it. Who knows where this could lead? You're all family now."

Marilyn replied, "All of you have been magicians. Al found our son. Doctor Generelli put him back together and Reilly and Maria protected him and gave him a life."

"We always dream of good outcomes," said Alastair, "sometimes we even get one!"

Chapter 33

The following week, Henry McArdle from Baker, Bright & Colson called.

"It's settled, Al, the quarrymen accepted the offer from Mid-Atlantic. Money will start moving this week. I'll need a detailed invoice from you for all the work done. Also, your associate Randy. I'll call Professor McGinn today and ask him for an invoice also."

"I wonder if you have to let the university know about the service he provided?" asked Alastair.

"I've been thinking about that. I'll ask the professor. I suspect he has to let the university know he was providing a service outside of his teaching responsibilities. I doubt they would make a claim on any part of the payment. Most likely, they want to make sure they are comfortable with the organization he was working with."

"You mean United Aliens for World Domination could be a cause for concern?" laughed Alastair.

"Something like that."

"What's going on with Trevor Durgan now? He seemed like a good guy caught up in the middle of all of this."

"Good question. I got a call from Floyd Gibson the other day. Mid-Atlantic wants to meet with Trevor. They are probably going to offer him compensation for all of his troubles. Floyd asked us to be co-counsel for the meeting. He's tied up in a big case in Philadelphia and asked us to the meeting so he can keep the momentum going. Our role will be more like his eyes and ears. In the end, it will be Floyd and Trevor who make the call on a settlement."

"So, at this point they're not suing?"

"That's right. We'll go see what Mid-Atlantic has to offer. Based on our settlements with the injured quarrymen, I don't think they'll try to play any games. I think they want to settle with Trevor quickly."

"You know, Al, you have a lot of continuity with this case. Join the meeting; you've got the history with all of this, especially Trevor's role. I'll come back to you with the time and date."

"Sure, give me a bit of advance notice. Things are starting to pile up here."

Alastair and Chantal spent most of the remainder of the day strategizing the upcoming insurance case. It seems a small, local company without any meaningful source of revenue had been filing claims for damages with three insurance companies. This had been going on for a number of years. Finally, one of the companies took notice. They were certain the claims were fraudulent and wanted to build a case. It was odd to Chantal how they could have gotten away with this for so long. Insurance companies were very cautious and always tracked their settlements. It appears that they were double-dipping on the three policies. How did these bad boys stay under their radar?

When Randy called in, they briefed him on the status. "Guys, we need to find out how they did this," laughed Randy, "could be a new line of business for us. Chantal can file claims in her spare time!"

"Oh, boy!" responded Chantal, you guys can visit me in jail!"

The meeting with Mid-Atlantic took place the following week. As before Barry Altmore was their lead. They only had their company attorney with them this time. No outside counsel.

Henry McArdle met with Trevor ahead of the meeting. "Trevor, this is an information gathering meeting. Let's hear what they have to say. I'm sure they'll put an offer on the table. We'll listen to it and make sure we understand it. After that, it's up to you and Floyd to make the call. I won't make any counter offers today. If I have any thoughts about their offer, I'll pass them to Floyd. I don't think this will be a contentious meeting but if it does go in that direction, keep cool and don't hit back. You're in the driver's seat, not Mid-Atlantic. If you want to take a break so we can talk, let me know."

Henry met the Mid-Atlantic team at the reception and took them back to their main conference room. Trevor was in the room nursing a cup of coffee. Although Trevor was an established customer, this was their first time meeting him.

Barry Altmore opened the meeting. "Trevor, I want to apologize for all the grief we've caused you. Our manufacturing process was broken, and we did not realize we had a problem until the accident at the quarry. The process is now fixed, and we are closely monitoring our product output. We have new equipment and new quality control steps in place. As I'm sure you know, we reached a settlement with the injured quarrymen. We want to also reach a settlement with you and avoid a lengthy court proceeding."

Trevor was not sure what to say at this point. He looked over to Henry McArdle for guidance.

"It's okay, Trevor," said Henry, "tell Mr. Altmore how this affected you."

"Mr. Altmore, when the explosion happened, I was terrified. It was like Iraq all over again. Noise, confusion, and debris raining down on those men. All I could think of was what had I done? The fact that the detonation did not blow out in my direction did not register with me until much later. I was a lot closer than the quarrymen. If the blast had come my way, it would have killed me for sure. What continues to trouble me is that Mid-Atlantic left me swinging in the wind. No contact from your company. I called numerous times to find out what might have happened and nobody, not one person, would return my calls. I wasn't trying to lay blame on anyone. This was a bad accident.

All of us needed to understand what happened and more importantly, how to fix it."

The company attorney attempted to speak but Trevor cut him off sharply.

"I have the floor, sir! After the accident, it was almost three weeks before anyone spoke to me. Mid-Atlantic had no interest in me. No interest to find out what I thought. I was a leper as far as you were concerned, and I think you were hoping that I was some cowboy who didn't know what he was doing. Then it would be problem solved for Mid-Atlantic! The only people who really cared to talk to me about the accident were Mr. Stewart and Professor McGinn. It's sort of comical when you think about it. They were retained by Baker, Bright & Colson and were determining if they should sue me. And they did! But in the conversations with them it was clear that they wanted to find out what happened, not throw accusations at the wall and hope something sticks. Mid-Atlantic may have ultimately stepped up to the problem but in the early stages, your response was pathetic. As we GIs used to say in the Army, ducking and dodging. Now that this is behind me, I still have a mixed feeling. Relief that it's over and my professional reputation is restored, but I'm still angry with Mid-Atlantic. This could have possibly gone against me and it would take years to clear my name."

When Trevor finished the room was quiet. The Mid-Atlantic company attorney attempted to comment but Barry Altmore raised his hand to silence him.

"Give me a few minutes to absorb Mr. Durgan's comments."

Henry was sitting next to Trevor and could see that his breathing was rapid. This had been an emotional experience for him. He reached over and put his hand on Trevor's forearm to reassure him and offer some comfort. The room remained silent. It was clear that they were waiting for Barry Altmore to respond. Barry was looking at Trevor who sat quietly looking at his hands. After some time, the two men made eye contact.

Barry replied, "You're right, everything you said is true. We failed you and were in denial during the early stages. There's no excuse for our conduct. An apology is so hollow. I don't really know what words can provide you with any closure. On a personal level, I am sincerely sorry and embarrassed by the performance of Mid-Atlantic. We would like to issue a formal letter of apology to you and if you want to go public with it, we won't contest it. Additionally, we'd like to offer you a payment of three-hundred thousand dollars. I hope you'll consider our offer."

Trevor was surprised. It seemed like a fair offer, maybe more than fair. He looked over at Henry for guidance.

"I'll need to consult with Trevor's attorney of record, Floyd Gibson. Can you put the offer in writing? I'll get with Floyd. I'd suggest something be drafted here today and I'll take it from there. Floyd and Trevor will make the decision."

"Henry," replied Barry, "I don't have a clock on the offer, but I do request that we communicate in a timely manner. I'd like to close this chapter out."

"I understand, I'll call you and we'll follow up in writing."

When the Mid-Atlantic team left, a draft of the compensation letter had been produced. Trevor and Henry sat in his office reviewing the details."

"What do you think, Henry?" asked Trevor.

"Candidly, better than I anticipated. God knows Mid-Atlantic screwed up, but they want to put this right. I can't speak for Floyd but I think he'll be happy with it. The fact that you weren't hurt makes me a bit cautious about going to trial. My opinion is that this is a good outcome. Let's call Floyd."

Henry and Floyd spoke about the compensation letter from Mid-Atlantic later that day. They quickly agreed to accept the offer. Henry called Barry Altmore to let him know of their acceptance and as promised, followed up with a letter. Case closed! Trevor received payment and a letter from Mid-Atlantic absolving him of any complicity in the accident. The letter was important because over time, he would be remembered as the guy who blew out the side of the quarry at the Bellmore farm. His reputation was solid with all the quarry owners, but the letter could have value down the road.

This closed out a painful chapter for Trevor, one he would not soon forget. It was a good outcome. He had his life and business back!

Epilogue

So, finally all the pieces had come together. It was hard to imagine that these events could be related in any capacity. You certainly couldn't see it going in. A young lad sees a horrific crime and runs away. A private investigator is retained to find him and in the process, closes out a painful chapter in his life. Along the way, he found the world's greatest dog—Sherlock!

So many things had happened in the space of a year. Alastair thought about this a lot. If he had not found Raymond, he would never have found Emi and the baby's killer. If he had not been involved in the quarry accident investigation, he never would have found Sherlock. He often thought, *Who's driving this bus? Not me, that's for sure. Someone has a strong hand in my life.*

Raymond continues to make good progress. He and Reilly are frequent visitors to Binghamton. When they come to town, Marilyn always makes a point of inviting Alastair and of course Sherlock over to dinner. Normally, when you close a case, you lose contact with the clients. Not that you avoid them, but it's rare to develop a close personal relationship. This case was certainly different. Alastair genuinely liked the two men and always looked forward to their visits. Sherlock was always happy to see her NBF (new best friend) Raymond.

Trevor Durgan continues to operate his blasting service around the northeast Pennsylvania area. With a senior in high school and a junior at Penn State, the settlement money is a welcome help to cover educational expenses. Maybe a new truck in there also!

Chantal is now spending full time on investigative work. Randy thinks it's a hoot when they work a case together. The dynamic duo rules! Finding Raymond and the quarry accident were major cases for Endwell Investigations. They took the agency to the next level. They are now getting calls from potential clients outside of the New York area.

Sherlock continues her role as the chief office greeter. She has put more than one nervous client at ease with her wagging tail!

Rocco Lanza died a few weeks after Alastair visited him at the hospice in Teaneck. He sent his granddaughter a condolence card. She loved her grandpa and with a bit of luck will never know about his real life. Alastair thought a lot about Rocco after he died. He wondered about his feelings. Happy he was dead? A feeling of revenge for his brutal killing of Emi and the baby? It was hard to sort out. He called Marty Fitzgerald at The Samaritan Counseling Center and set up an appointment. He was not stressed about his mixed feelings but wanted to better understand what was going on. In the end, putting emotions aside, it was a relief. Pure joyous relief!

A long-open chapter in his life was finally closed. He didn't realize how it had stayed with him over the years. Always there below the surface. Now he didn't have to carry the painful memories anymore.

Other books by FJ Donohue
Up State Mystery series
(Cozy Mysteries set in update New York)

Hit and Run https://books2read.com/u/b5val6

Closure https://books2read.com/u/mejkO9

Right Time Wrong Place https://books2read.com/u/md7MWd

Two Murders by the River https://books2read.com/u/4jAZ7X

The Caribbean Laundry https://books2read.com/u/mYZdlo

A Serial Killer Returns https://books2read.com/u/bPy11z

The Snowbird Bank Robber https://books2read.com/u/mvoV68

About the author:

I'm a retired International Sales Director, having worked in the commercial and military flight simulation industry for over 30 years. I lived in Brussels (Belgium) and Bonn (Germany) for eight years and met my British wife in Brussels. Before my career in the flight simulation industry, I was an Armaments and Electronics Maintenance Officer in the USAF during the Viet Nam era conflict. We have three children and seven grandchildren.

Since retirement I continue to chase an ever-elusive golf game.

Home is a small town in central New York State where the novellas are set.

I'm a volunteer mediator and Lemon Law arbitrator and this occasionally appears in the stories. An underlying theme in my novellas is people helping people. In spite of the difficulties and crime that may surround us, there is always hope in friendship and good neighbors.

Go to my website below for information about my novellas and to contact me for a FREE short story. I won't use your information for any other purpose.

https://upstatemysteries.godaddysites.com/

Also by fj donohue

Endwell Investigations
Full Circle

Upstate Mystery
Hit and Run
Two Murders by the River
A Serial Killer Returns
Right Time Wrong Place
The Caribbean Laundry

Upstate Mystery #2
Closure

Upstate Mystery #7
The Snowbird Bank Robber

About the Author

I'm a retired International Sales Director, having worked in the commercial and military flight simulation industry for over 30 years. I lived in Brussels (Belgium) and Bonn (Germany) for eight years and met my British wife in Brussels. Before my career in the flight simulation industry, I was an Armaments and Electronics Maintenance Officer in the USAF during the Viet Nam era conflict. We have three children and seven grandchildren.

Since retirement I continue to chase an ever-elusive golf game.

Home is a small town in central New York State where the novellas are set.

I'm a volunteer mediator and Lemon Law arbitrator and this occasionally appears in the stories. An underlying theme in my novellas is people helping people. In spite of the difficulties and crime that may surround us, there is always hope in friendship and good neighbors.

Go to my website below for information about my novellas and to contact me for a FREE short story. I won't use your information for any other purpose.

Read more at https://upstatemystery.com.